Prologue 1 the tale of the girl who loved to travel and wanted adventure, Minnesota 1971

In the early 1970's, it was a really cold day and a lot of snow was falling down on the ground. And it was a normal January day in 1971, But then there was a rich couple who were well dressed, the man had on a nice 1970's suit and tie, the wife had diamonds on the rings she was wearing, And then also the couple had 2 beautiful little girls. The oldest one had very golden hair and she had blue eyes, the other one had brown hair and had green eyes. And every time this couple went anywhere such as the mall or any fun places, the oldest girl in the family would love going places with her parents. And this girl was very curious about the world around her, and this girl really had big dreams for herself as well. She didn't really know what she wanted to do yet, but the little girl kept an open mind. The couple went back home and they stayed in a really nice house in a suburb in Minnesota. And the girls had a very wonderful childhood, the dad worked as a normal minimum wage job working at a Wendy's, he didn't really make much at his job, but however that being said, he would stop into his bank branch on the way home from work and meet with his banker and his banker would go over with him which companies to invest in. And with the paycheck he had, he would use his paycheck to find companies that didn't have a lot of value to their name and buy somewhere 600,000 stocks with that company. The girls would grow up and they right away be sent to college with money that their parents gave them. Both girls went to the University of Minnesota around the same time Alex went to University of Washington in 1980. Accept this girl was a little bite older then Alex. And she also worked for her parents before going to college as well.

But then as the girls got there, some of the roommates that they had were sadly not very good common sense people. And some of the roommates would always problems with the older girl going to gas stations and getting snacks and getting beer. And they even said at one point it was not very lady like. The girls also went to normal and really crazy college parties and there was people being silly and dancing to 1980's music and people wearing a lot of 1980's clothes and having crazy 1980's fashions. And also people were drinking some drinks, some people were watching TV, playing pool or playing darts. And then other crazy people were playing beer pong as well. The girl was then at the party and she was drinking a coke and eating a hot dog. But then as they were, there was also another gentlemen at the party and he looked very little but also very athletic at the same time and he was drinking a beer. And the girl saw him and started flirting with him. "Hey sweetie, this is a great party" she said "Oh yeah it's a really wonderful and a really wild party" he said "Oh yeah I agree" she said "I'm Spencer by the way" Spencer said "I'm Sadie" Sadie said "So what brings you to this wild little place?" Spencer asked "Well my sister and I found out that there was going to be party here and we came" Sadie said "Oh that's awesome" Spencer said "So what do you do when your not going to school?"

Spencer asked "Well I actually work at Penny Mora's here in the city" Sadie said, "Oh that's a great store, I hear they are just like Nordstrom's in Seattle, I hear on the news that place is getting really good" Spencer said "Oh yeah I have herd that too" Sadie said "So what are you studying Spencer?" Sadie asked "So far…. nothing…At least not yet anyway" Spencer said "Well for me I do like to travel, and I do want to be a traveling personality and share my adventures to the world" Sadie said "Well that's really ballsy baby girl" Spencer said "I know…" Sadie said and then Sadie smiled at Spencer. And then during that night, they both got to know each other very well and right away the two had a lot in common, and they both wanted to travel and see the world. And then in the same night, Spencer and Sadie were making out in Spencer's dorm around the University of Minnesota campus. And all of a sudden in the coming months, Sadie and Spencer flunked out of school and the three people started working very different jobs. Sadie worked at the same job and she also told her boss about the plan and her boss was all in as well. Sadie's sister April would also be part of this adventure of hers in making a TV program where they talked about traveling and going places as well. And Sadie using the knowledge from her mom and dad, started investing in the stock market as the economy is getting really good. And Sadie bought a lot of stocks from small companies and in one year alone, she got around $900,000 in shares and Spencer would invest even more then Sadie would around 900$ and then getting 9,000,000$ in shares.

And from there, they just really wanted to move somewhere else. And both Sadie and Spencer decided to move to Seattle, Washington. And they moved into a really fancy house that was in the Seattle area that had a swimming pool and a hot tub, a gym, and also a huge basement where there was a big TV room and video game room as well. That, and also a bar where there was a lot of alcohol as well. And from 1980 to 1989 and started recording on their adventures on an old video camera from the 1980's. And they went to a lot of places all over the world such as in Europe and went to a lot of countries such as Italy, England, France, New Zealand, and also go to Mexico, Brazil, and then to Ireland and then to Australia. And then she also traveled around the United States of America as well. And then there would be times where also explored Canada and all the territories in that country as well. But whenever Sadie, Spencer, and April went anywhere, they always were really smart; they also made sure not to spend a lot of money as well. And then also make sure they were around safe people as well. And by the late 80's her popularity and her fame really grew a lot. And when Sadie, April, and Spencer returned to the states, she then was called on the phone to go on a radio show in San Diego. And when she was on the radio, she was really happy, really bubbly, and she just really loved to laugh as well. And not only that, but she also answered her questions correctly as well.

But then also on that same day Sadie was on the radio, Alex was coming back from working at Seattle agencies going over reports and then attending gun practice. And as Alex was driving home in downtown Seattle and heading to his apartment, he then was listening to Sadie on the radio and explaining her adventures and how she has able to travel the world on a budget. Alex right way from listening to her on the radio, loved her voice and thought in his little brain "Ah yeah she is a very beautiful and a very gorgeous and a very stunning and a very sexy baby girl" Alex said and thought as he was driving home, and then as Alex came home from Seattle Agencies, he then took a shower and he was only wearing a T-shirt and boxer underwear and not wearing any pants as well. And then all of a sudden, Alex started making an ice coffee and then he also put whipped cream on the coffee and then Alex was able to make something to eat as well. And then Alex turned on TV and he started slipping through the channels. And sometimes Alex really does not take the little tiny local channels seriously and he mostly focuses on the sports channels and also the higher channels as well. But as Alex was flipping through, he then saw Sadie's show on TV and it was on channel 5 and the show was called "Living Adventures with Sadie" and Sadie spoke and it was mostly set up like a normal talk show but with traveling and the show always started out with a bing and then some music would play and then the crowd would start clapping and making a lot of noise "Hi everyone this is Sadie on Living adventures and I do this program everyday Wednesday. And my goodness it is really great to be back. And today I got to go to Germany, and we will have clips of that real soon. And we will have a guest on the show very soon as well" Sadie said and then as Alex kept on watching, he was also really amazed at how beautiful and gorgeous, and very stunning and very happy and she just loved to laugh a lot. And she also wore a lot of really beautiful and really gorgeous 1980's style dresses on her show. And then Alex was really amazed at how beautiful and athletic her body was. And then Alex kept on thinking "Ah wow she is super pretty and very beautiful and damn she is fine" Alex thought in his head and from there, Alex was hooked on Sadie's TV show about traveling and talking about her adventures and also having special guests on the show as well. And every time Alex didn't have any missions from 1984 to 1988 Alex always watched Sadie doing her TV shows. And whenever Alex heard the bell noise on TV, he really knew something was about to go down and Alex always had popcorn with cheese zits under the piles of popcorn and also some goldfish and cheese related snacks under the popcorn. And then he would drink a lot of junk drinks such as soda, beer, a milkshakes, icey's, and the list goes on and on of junk drinks and junk food.

And then there would even be times when Michael and Tony would come over to watch Sadie's show on TV. And as they were watching the show, they were watching an episode on her program were she went to Russia. And this episode was a lot of more serious because she was interviewing someone who was an Indian-American who was a young ambassador to Russia. And his name Salem Suyog Jadon. And the man was really muscular and he had dark skin and he also had black hair as well. But he spoke really well with an American accent. And Salem was talking about Russia and how the berlin wall could fall at any point after Reagan's speech in Berlin. And then there was also a much important detail in that interview as well where Salem said he was going to do a rally in Portland, Oregon to rally behind President Regan and also rally behind America as well against the Communist. "Alright yes defiantly well this was Living Adventures With Sadie. And I will see you guys next time" Sadie said and then the episode ended.

And back the studio around in downtown Seattle, Salem was leaving the building and he was heading to his house that was around the University of Washington neighborhood. But then as he went to sleep that night, there was a lot of evil Sandinistas from Nicaragua that were spying on him. And not only that, but they also had contact with more Sandinista groups that were in the United States including in Portland, Oregon as well. And the next day, Salem got up and he took a shower and he got into his car and he started driving to Portland, Oregon and it was around a 2-hour drive. But as he got to the city, he then stayed in a really fancy hotel. And once he was checked in, around that same point, once Alex saw Salem on TV, he knew that Salem in some way was going to be in grave danger because Alex knew from being in Portland back in 1976 when he was 16, he knew there a lot of anti-America people that refuged to that part of the country just like did with San Francisco and anything that supports an anti-America agenda, those evil people would go there. The next day, Alex went to Seattle agencies and he reported to Rivers saying that there might be an attack in Portland and wanted Rivers grant him approval to go on a mission there. And Rivers ended up saying yes. Alex also told him about Sadie's new show as well. And from there, Alex was on his way to Portland and Alex actually took the train to get there. And as Alex was on the train, he really thought about what he was going to run into. And he also knew he had to find Jadon before any bad people did.

Prologue 2 The Sandinistas and Borodina's attack at the pro America rally in Portland

As Alex got to Portland, He then got off the train and he took a bus that was heading to downtown Portland. As Alex was on the bus, he did notice a sign that said, "Support for the Berlin wall coming down" and then Alex also checked into a hotel as well. "Can I help you?" the hotel lady asked "yes the names Aussmen...Alex Aussmen...I would love to check into a hotel here" Alex said "Alright okay, we will get your room very soon" she said and then the lady was able to get Alex a hotel key and she was able to hand it to him "Here is your key sir" she said "thank you so much sweetie" Alex said and then Alex went to the elevator and he pressed on the 7th floor and the elevator started going up. Alex got off the elevator and he started heading to his hotel room. Alex set his bags on his bed and Alex started changing out of his suit and tie and started putting on normal 1980's style clothes. Alex was able to get out of his hotel room and he started heading more towards a park area that was is around a couple of department stores. Alex then kept on walking and he saw Salem go into a bar that was inside of Nordstrom. Alex went into the Nordstrom and he saw Salem getting a beer and also drinking shots before speaking. Alex then walked up to that same bar counter and he didn't really get any beer he just got water and was eating some pistachio nuts. And then while he was there, Alex then saw more alcoholic drinks and he started mentally writing notes in his head and writing down and memorizing every alcohol brand that there is. And then Salem turned to Alex and then turned away from him and then Alex turned to him "Today is a great night for a speaking rally" Alex said "oh yeah defiantly we need to get the Berlin wall to come down" Salem said "wait, my man, you watched my interview with Sadie" Salem asked "Yeah I did. I'm Alex Aussmen, private investigator. And I believe you maybe in danger" Alex said "What do you mean dude?" Salem said, "I'm saying that a lot of anti-America people live here in Portland and they always support a lot of anti-America causes and they come here" Alex said "But doesn't that happen in Seattle as well?" Salem asked "it does but we have a lot of business people in Seattle and Seattle has a lot going for it" Alex said "let me at least come with you to the rally" Alex said "Alright okay be my guess man" Salem said and then as Salem was done drinking his beer. Alex and Salem started walking to the rally and at the rally; Alex saw a lot of people wearing T-shirts in supporting George H.W. Bush and people had a lot of American flag T-shirts. And people were going crazy and wissleling and making a lot more crazy sounds as well. And then Salem started walking up to the podium "Good evening everyone, it is my pleasure to be here. And really soon we are going to create peace in Russia and the Berlin wall will come down. And we don't want socialism or communism getting into our country. And we don't want to be like everyone else, we want to be the United States of America. And when Reagan is out, we must support a candidate that will continue the path of patriotism and the free market and also the rule of law as well. And we must end socialism and communism once and for all" Salem said and a lot of the people there roaring and clapping and chanting "USA, USA, USA, USA, USA!!!!!!!!" and but then all of a sudden as Alex was listening to the speech, he saw a lot of Hispanics that were wearing black and red suit and ties and sun glasses. And then he also saw some evil people in blue and yellow tuxedos. And then all of a sudden an evil huge mob of evil Ukraine and Sandinista thugs showed up and created a riot and a huge fight broke out and also gunfire broke out as well. And everyone was going crazy.

And then a lot of Sandinistas and Ukraine thugs started attacking and shooting at people. All of a sudden, Alex took out a PP7 gun and he started firing 30 bullets at them "LA RAZA!!!!!, LA RAZA!!!!!, LA RAZA!!!!!!!, LA RAZA!!!!!!! MATA EL GRINGO!!!!!!!" They yelled in Spanish and then Alex grunted his teeth in anger and was very pissed off and he started firing 300 bullets at 60 Sandinista thugs coming at him with riffle guns. Alex then took cover and he hid behind objects and he kept on shooting and then one of the Sandinista thugs tried to tackle Alex, but Alex was able to dodge the tackle and he punched the thug in the face and then dodged another attack and kicked another Sandinista in the balls, and then another one tried to stab Alex with a machete knife, Alex then dodged the machete attacks and Alex punched the Sandinista thug in the face and grabbed him and slammed him into a car.

And then Alex started running and he grabbed Salem "come on we have to get out of here" Alex said "who are these fucking people?!..." Salem said, "They are the communist down in Nicaragua, they are the Sandinistas, and they are just as evil as the communist in Russia" Alex said and then Alex and Salem hid behind a car and Alex took out another gun and he loaded up his gun and started shooting 90 bullets at them and Alex was able to kill 40 Sandinistas thugs and shoot them in the head and also shoot them in the neck. And then Salem saw a lot of Sandinista thugs were coming close at them and shooting A33 riffles at Alex, Alex kept on shooting at them.

And then Alex and Salem started running and they started running and Alex saw a early 1980's car and Alex was able to break into the car and Salem was riding shot-gun. "Hold on" Alex said and then the Ukraine thugs started coming at them as well "Ne dozvoljajte amerykans'komu pity!!!!!!!" The Ukraine thugs yelled and then Alex put the pedal to the medal and he started driving the car really fast. Alex drove the car really fast all over Downtown Portland and Alex kept on taking four different turns. And then Alex was going around 500 miles per hour and then more Sandinistas and Ukraine thugs kept on chasing after Alex as Alex was going really fast. "LA RAZA!!!!!!!, LA RAZA, LA RAZA, LA RAZA!!!!!!!!" the Sandinistas kept on yelling at Alex "Vamos a llevarnos de vuelta a Nicaraguia por todos los crímenes que cometieron a nuestro país, el Senior Aussmen!!!!!" they yelled "Yeah fuck all of you!!!!!!" Alex yelled and then Alex was able to find a bomb in his pocket and then Alex threw the bomb at the other cars that were chasing Alex and then the car exploded into flames and caught on fire and then more thugs started firing more bullets at Alex. Alex then kept on taking sharp turns and then as he was driving, Alex then loaded up PP7 gun and Alex kept on firing bullets at the Sandinistas. And then as Alex was going really fast and going around 900 miles per hour, a lot of Sandinistas that were black and red helicopters started chasing after Alex and firing a lot of advanced missiles and causing a lot of explosions and more buildings and cars were catching on fire and Alex kept on driving with a lot of energy in his little right pinky. And then a lot of motorcycles with USSR flags started chasing Alex and they started rocket launchers at Alex, and then Alex dodging all of the rockets firing at him. Alex then took out his gun and Alex fired 50 bullets and reloading and shooting at the tires and shooting at their arms and causing them to crash in the process and more explosions happening. Alex kept on driving really fast and he ended up around the bridge by the Columbia River and by the Washington state boarder. And then Alex was driving and then he parked the car and drifted car really fast and then put the car on park. Alex then turned back to Salem "stay here man" Alex said and then Alex took out another pistol gun and he reloaded the gun with more bullets.

Alex then heard the motorcycles and more helicopters coming towards him. And then Alex took out his DD4 gun and Alex started shooting at the Ukraine thugs coming at him and shooting around 90 bullets at them. Alex then took out bombs and he was able to throw around 5 different grenades at a lot of Sandinista thugs that were coming at him at a rapid pace. And then Alex kept on running and he saw one of the ropes. Alex jumped on to one of the ropes and Alex started climbing up the top of the rope and Alex was able to get to the top and the Sandinistas helicopters kept on shooting at Alex. Alex was able to dodge the bullets and Alex saw a rocket launcher and Alex picked up the rocket launcher and Alex with careful aim and holding on to the launcher very tight. And as the Sandinistas were coming after Alex in very intense fashion and at a really fast race, Alex then shot around 3 rockets at the Sandinista helicopters and Alex was able to blow up 5 different Sandinista helicopters as well "El día de mayo vamos a bajar. Nos han golpeado!!!!" The Sandinistas inside of the helicopters yelled and then there was a huge explosion and the helicopter landed in the Columbia River and killed the Sandinistas inside of the helicopter. And then Alex climbed off of the bridge and he was able to get back on the ground and Alex saw a lot of motorcycles that had a lot of Ukraine and USSR flags coming at Alex. "MY tebe teper pan AUSSMEN!!!!!!!!!!" They yelled and then Alex grunted his teeth and Alex started firing 10 different rockets at the Ukraine thugs and causing a lot of explosions and their motorcycles caught on fire. And then the thugs flew off of the motorcycles off the bridge and into the water. And then more thugs started coming at Alex and shooting at them, Alex was able to dodge the attacks and then the thugs turned back and Alex reloaded the rocket launcher and fired another rocket back at the Ukraine thug and blew them up in flames and smoke. And then another van full of Sandinistas thugs waving the Sandinista flag "Te tenemos ahora Señor Aussmen!!!!!" they yelled and then they started throwing a lot of bombs at Alex and then Alex started running away from the vans and Alex and they started firing a lot of bullets at Alex. Alex then jumped on another rope that was on the bridge and Alex took out another gun and reloaded the gun and Alex started shooting at the tires and then Alex grunted his teeth and Alex shot at one of the Sandinista thugs in the van and killing two of them as well. And then the Sandinista thugs came out of the car and they started shooting at Alex. Alex was able to do a summersault and dodge the bullets coming at him and he was able to take out another gun and reload the gun and Alex started shooting around 300 bullets at the Sandinista thugs and shooting them in the head and in the neck and also in the chest as well. And then the van was rolling on the bridge and drifting and then all of a sudden, the Sandinista thug van started going in the air and turning in circles. And then it landed on the ground and it crashed on the ground and then Alex started running to the van with the rocket launcher in his hands. "Who sent you?!...." Alex yelled in a very angry voice "We will get you and take you back one of these days gringo!!!!" the Sandinista thugs said "Yeah like fuck that is going to happen" Alex yelled in anger and then all of a sudden out of the shadows more Sandinista and Ukraine thugs showed up as Victoria Borodina showed up again "Making fire piles Zero, Zero One?!...." Victoria said and she is wearing a red and black jumpsuit with Blue and yellow boots and also one part of her hair was blue and blonde, and the other half was died red and black "One of these days, I will capture you Alex and torture you in Nicaragua and run away as much you want little boy, but I will always be better" Victoria said "I'm not running Victoria, I am protecting an innocent person from being killed by one of your thugs!!!!" Alex said "very well then little boy!!!!" Victoria said and then Victoria took out a remote and she pressed a button on it and then all of a sudden, a lot of metal arms started growing out of her watches that she was wearing and the metal claws tried to grab Alex, Alex then grunted his teeth and he was able to throw 6 different punches at the arms. And then Alex was able to use a flame thrower gadget to burn the metal arms that Victoria Borodina had, then she took out a king staff and she tried to whack Alex in the face and she threw around 14 different staff attacks and Alex was able to dodge all 14 of them. And then Alex kicked Borodina in the stomach and then Borodina recovered from the attack and she whacked Alex in the face and then she grabbed a very hot glove to try to burn Alex's face "This is going to cause a really huge sting to your face Little boy!!!!!!!..." Victoria said as she was grabbing Alex by the neck and then Alex kicked her in the face with both of his legs and then Alex saw the rocket launcher and he picked up the rocket launcher and Alex all of a sudden, fired a rocket out of the rocket launcher and he shot Victoria Borodina in the stomach and then she started yelling and there was a huge explosion in flames and then Alex ran to the ledge of the river and saw parts of the fire go into river "Welcome to hell Borodina!!!!!" Alex yelled and then all of a sudden, Alex turned back and he saw Borodina's little Rottweiler dog growling and making a lot of evil and nasty and very mean dog barks at Alex. And then from there even though the dog didn't attack or bite Alex, he did notice something was not right and he knew that this time in fighting Victoria Borodina that he knew he was going to need more help and if Alex learned anything from the past, it's that Victoria Borodina is a lot like the evil and creepy and nasty monster that children are afraid of and is like the monster under the bed that can crawl up and snatch you and kidnap you and torture you and overall kill you as well.

Alex was able to leave Portland and he was able to take Salem back to his hotel room in Portland. But as this was happening, all of a sudden, there was communist submarine that was able to find Borodina and Borodina looked very beat up from fighting Alex, and all of a sudden the doctors inside the submarine started operating on Victoria and all of a sudden, they put her through plastic surgery and her skin started getting wrinkled, she started growing a lot of zits on her face, her hair started turning gray and white behind all of the hair dye that she put into it. And then also Victoria's teeth were getting yellow and ugly and also starting to turn black as well and started gaining wrinkles around her eyes some of her face as well. And then as the operation was completed, Borodina stood up and her hands were all wrinkled and old and her finger nails were dirty and smelly and had a lot of dirt and bacteria in them "Mirror!!!!!" Borodina yelled and then one of the Ukraine soldiers gave her the mirror and then Borodina broke the mirror and she broke the glass on the mirror "Ms. Borodina, I'm really sorry that you look very ugly, we tired to do the best that we could..." the solider said and then all of a sudden very aggressively she grabbed the solider by the neck and start chocking him very badly and her nails were stabbing him and a lot of blood was coming out his neck and Victoria was able to kill him and she threw him to the floor. "YOU FUCKING FOOL, YOU RUINED MY BEAUTY AND YOU RUINED MY STUNNING LOOKS!!!!!!" Borodina said in a very creepy and very witch like voice "BUT SOON I WILL TAKE OVER THE WORLD AND SOON I WILL BECOME EVEN MORE RICH AND NOT ONLY WILL I USE THE MONEY TO BECOME BEAUITFUL AGAIN, I WILL USE TO FUND THE SANDINSTAS AND THE SOVIET UNION AND MY PLAN WILL BE VERY SIMPLE!!!!!!!!....I WILL FIND A RICH PERSON IN AMERICA AND KILL THAT PERSON, STEEL THEIR MONEY AND THEIR FORTUNE JUST LIKE I DID EMILY ROMNEY AND SABRINA FIORINA AND THEN JUST LIKE I DID WITH AGNET PAUL MILLAT AS WELL!!!!!!!!!...AND THIS TIME I WILL SUCCED AND I WILL KILL ALEX AUSSMEN ZERO, ZERO ONE ONCE AND FOR ALL!!!!!!!!!" Victoria said and then Victoria looked a magazine and she then saw Sadie on the magazine "oh that will be perfect to kidnap a TV host on a talk show and ruin her and destroy her life and steel all of her fortune and kill her boyfriend...and I will get that pretty girl and use her DNA as well. And as for Alex Aussmen, I will get you this time little boy!!!!!!!!....AND NOTHING CAN TRULY STOP ME

NOW!!!!!!!!!!.....EHEHEHEHEHEHEHEHEHEHEHEHEHEHEHEHEHEHEHEHEHE
HEHEHEHEHEHEHEHEHEHEHEHEHEHEHEHEHEHEHEHEHEHE.....MUAHAHAHAH
AHAHAHAHAHAHAHAHAHAHAHAHAHAHAHAHAHAHAHAHAHAHAHAHAHAHAHA
HAHAHAHAHAHAHAHAHAHA
BRAHAAHAHAHAHAHAHAHAHAHAHAHAHAHAHAHAHAHAHAHAHAHAHAHAHAA
HAHAHAHAHAHAHAHAHAHAHAHAHAHAHAHAHAHAHAHAHAHAHAHAHAHAHA
HAHAHAHAHAHAHAHAHAHAHAHAHAHAHAHAHAHAHAHAHAHAHAHAHA...E
HEHEHEHEHEHEHEHEHEHEHEHEHEHE
AHAHAHAHAAHAHAHAHAHAHAHAHAHAHAHAHAHAHAHAHAHAHAHHAHA
MUAHAHAHAHAHAHAHAHAHAHAHAHAHAHAHAHAHAHAHAHAHAHAHAHAHAH
AHAHAHAHA!!!!!!!!!!!!!!!!!!!!!" Victoria laughed and then as Victoria was laughing,
parts of herself was reveled and there was thunder and lighting outside and Victoria
kept on looking at the picture of Sadie in the magazine and the whole room was
turning dark and there was more thunder and lighting as well.

Chapter 1 A Big surprise in Ballard, Seattle, Washington 1989

As the sun was rising in downtown Seattle, there is a special place in the heart of
Seattle and it's a neighborhood or a borough, as some people from the east coast
would call it. And the name of this neighborhood was Ballard, the neighborhood is
really known for a lot of fishermen boats and a lot of fishermen going up to Alaska
and getting a lot of fish and crap and also some shrimp as well. But it's really
important to know that Alex was able to get released out of the hospital in
downtown Seattle after the attacks that he in Washington DC. Alex was released
from the hospital and there were two people that picked up Alex and those people
were Tony and Michael. And as Alex was released from the hospital, Michael and
Tony took Alex to get some lunch and they took him out for fish and chips and they
took him to a restaurant called Anthony's. And from there, Alex was eating fine once
again and he was also drinking his soda just like he would drink any other drink.
"How do you feel Alex?" Michael asked him "Sadly I feel very light-headed and my
brain feels like complete dog-shit" Alex said "Yeah I'm sorry to hear about that home
boy, I mean I have been watching the news, and yeah hommie those Sandinistas in
that country are just very awful people" Tony said "Did you find anything else about
them?" Alex said "well...not really it's just another mission of me attacking them and
blowing up parts of their country and them yelling at me and saying a lot of racist
things at me" Alex said "oh dear yikes I'm sorry Alex" Michael said "Hey you don't
have to be sorry buddy" Alex said and then all of a sudden, the food came and Alex,
Michael, and Tony started eating the food and munching all of it like big husky dogs
eating a bone. And then they also drank 4 big shots and gulps of soda and felt very
hyper and very silly as well.

They then were able to take Alex home back to his pen house apartment in
downtown Seattle. As Alex got home, he then started all the things that were
mentioned in the prologue especially with him starting to watch Sadie and her
boyfriend and her sister on TV, and then also the events of him going to Portland,
Oregon. And then also before that, Alex was going to Seattle agencies but he just

didn't have missions assigned to him and he there for gun practice, working out at the facility weather it was him swimming in the pool, working out and doing cardio workouts or also lifting weights as well. Alex also had a sheet of paper recording every single set and every workout stat. And everyday Alex ended up burring around 1,000 calories a day. And then as he was done working out, he would also be studying other agent reports coming in and also writing stuff down and taking notes on the blue prints handed to him. And then also Alex would go to meetings and listen to other operative officials talk about missions that were coming up even though he was not assigned to go on those missions. And then also one day as Alex was swimming, he then saw Jenny in a very beautiful and a very gorgeous and very stunning and a very sexy 1980's bikini bathing suit and she had a very beautiful and a very gorgeous smile on her face. "Hey Alex, I didn't know you were coming here for a swim?" Jenny said and then as Alex saw her and as he was getting done swimming his 100th lap in the pool, Alex then got out of the pool and since Alex was not seeing anyone, Alex just started walking up to Jenny and started making out with Jenny by the pool and Alex gave her a really smooch on the lips and also Alex started touching her. "You doing anything later today?" Alex asked "no...I'm not...I'm all yours" Jenny said, "oh I love the sound of that baby girl" Alex said and then after Alex was done swimming, Alex and Jenny took showers and they got dressed and they were wearing really cool looking 1980's clothes. And then Alex softly put his arms around jenny and Jenny had a really big smile on her face "So where were you. I haven't seen you in a while" Jenny said "I was on in a mission in Nicaragua and also in Washington DC as well" Alex said "oh that sounds really exciting, I really wish I can come with you on all those missions Alex, Rivers just has me doing office work all the time and I have never really been anywhere" Jenny said "you were on my last local mission that was in Bellevue" Alex said "Oh that's right I forgot" Jenny said "So where are we going tonight?" Jenny said, "I actually really didn't know, we can go to a fancy restaurant in Seattle, and then come back to my apartment, does that sound like a great idea?" Alex asked "Oh that is a fantastic idea Alex" Jenny said and then Alex raised his left hand and a taxi car showed up and Alex and Jenny got into the car. "Where to?" the driver asked "Any fancy place in Seattle" Alex said, "yes sir" the driver said

The taxi driver started taking Alex and Jenny to a fancy restaurant in downtown Seattle. And the driver dropped them off and they got out of the car and started heading into the restaurant. Alex and Jenny were able to get seated and they sat upstairs and had a view of the Seattle skyline from their table. "Wow this is really wonderful Alex, this is the first time you have actually took me on a date" Jenny said "Well I am really glad you were free Jenny" Alex said "I just really can't believe I'm 29 years old, it just felt like yesterday I just became a secret agent all those years ago" Alex said "How did you become a secret agent?" Jenny asked Alex then paused for a little bit and then he was able to take a deep breath "it's kind of complicated" Alex said, "What do you mean Alex?" Jenny asked "well I am saying that how I became a secret agent was not a very normal way, you see Jenny, there are parts of my life that are very dark and very scary and also my life was never easy because my parents never thought I was going to be anything in life and basically treated me like I was nothing. And...I also ran away from them as well and I raised by a fortune teller as well" Alex said "That sounds really cool" Jenny said "it may be cool to you but I have done things and seen things that I am not proud of" Alex said "you can tell me Alex, were adults" Jenny said "okay well Jenny...I have just always a lot of people come after me and even a lot of evil and messed up people come after me" Alex said "Like what Alex?" Jenny said "I don't know like I know when I was 16 I had to go to creepy medical building in downtown Seattle with my guardian name Emmy Lewis and I had to get tested for disability. At least that is what was suppose to happen but instead I got hunted and I had run through an obstacle course and run through the building and swim in very cold water butt naked, it was not good" Alex said "Oh you poor baby" Jenny said "oh dear I'm sorry Alex" Jenny said "Are you okay personally Alex?" Jenny asked him "Yeah it's fine, I'm over it and it was many years ago. But my point is that I have a dark past and my life is very edgy and not very clean as well" Alex said "it's okay Alex, I understand, we all have dark things in our past" Jenny said and then Jenny put her right hand on Alex's hand and she started touching Alex and then from there, Alex started feeling a lot more relaxed and they eating the food that they ordered and then Alex was able to pay for Jenny and himself and pay the bill. And then from there, they started heading to his apartment.

And then as they got back to Alex's apartment, Jenny and Alex started making out and kissing each other on the lips and went into Alex's bedroom and started taking each other's clothes off. And then Alex landed on his bed and then Jenny kept making out with Alex on the bed and they started laughing "oh my" Jenny said and they passionately making love with each other. "Wahoooooooooo!!!!" Jenny said as Alex was making out with her and kissing her on the lips. And then they started making out and having sex for the remainder of the night. And then next day morning, Alex saw the sun rising up at around 7:30AM and as Alex was getting up, Jenny was sleeping on Alex's chest and she was kissing Alex's chest and then Jenny kissed Alex on the lips and then both of them were kissing each other. Alex then got up and he put a towel to cover up and Alex looked at the sun and he also looked at the Seattle skyline. And then Alex started heading to his bathroom and he turned on the water and the water started coming down on him. And then as Alex was in the shower, Jenny went into the shower with Alex and they started kissing and making out in the shower. For the rest of the morning, and then after they took a shower, Alex and Jenny started heading to breakfast and Alex paid breakfast and he made sure to tip the waiter that served both of them. "Anyway thank you so much for breakfast Alex" Jenny said "Your welcome Jenny" Alex said "Well I am really sad that I have to leave you but I think Rivers is sending me on another mission where I have to go to Europe and go on my first overseas mission" Jenny said "that sounds fantastic Jenny" Alex said and then Jenny got up from the chair and she walked over to Alex and she was able to give Alex a kiss on the check and she started walking to the door in her beautiful high heels and Alex just smiled as he was eyeing her, but trying to be clam and cool, Alex knew that at some point, he was going to be assigned a new mission from Rivers.

Alex then left the restaurant and since he really didn't have anything else on his calendar, he then started looking around downtown Seattle and he started going to a lot of stores. And as Alex was in downtown Seattle, a communist Russian in the city started fallowing Alex as he was in the stores, and as Alex was walking into a book store, Alex started looking at another different novels at the store, but then as Alex was reading, the same communist Russian thug and an anti-America guy with a T-shirt of him mocking president Reagan fallowed Alex as well. And little did Alex know, he was about to be in mortal danger. And then as Alex kept on reading, both of these guys came at Alex and notice his style of suit he was wearing "HEY FUCK REAGAN!!!!!!! FUCK YOU WHITE BOY!!!!!!!" the anti-America guy yelled at Alex and then the ugly looking young man got really upset and he started screaming and yelling and he also had a big sharp pocket knife and he threw 19 different knife attacks at Alex. Alex then right away jumped in the air and he landed on the ground and Alex started dodging the attacks that the anti-America guy was throwing at him. And then Alex dodged more attacks and then Alex kicked him in the face and then the guy tried to stab him in the chest and Alex got really aggressive and slammed anti-America guy against the wall and Alex grabbed his shoulder and Alex slammed his head against 5 glass windows and Alex grabbed a hard edge book slammed him from behind 7 times in the head. And then the ugly anti-America turned back and he threw more punches and more kicks at Alex and then he also bull-rushed at Alex and caused Alex to land on the ground "I'M GOING TO MAKE SURE YOU CONSERTIVES DIE IN A BURNING FIRE!!!!!!!" he yelled in complete anger and then Alex got up and then Alex dodged another attack and Alex punched him in the face and threw another kick at the attacker. And then the communist Russia wanted to kill Alex he took out a Russian sword and tried to stab and cut Alex and threw around 30 different attacks at Alex. Alex was able to dodge the attacks and then the communist Russian punched Alex in the face and Alex had a bloody lip and then both of the aggressive men tried to tackle Alex and then grabbed the Russian's wrist really hard and slammed him against the wall. And then he tried to attack Alex with Russian sword and then Alex punched the gun in the face was able to kill him. And then Alex was fighting the anti-America guy and he threw more punches and kicks at Alex. Alex kept on dodging the attacks and then did an upper cut punch at the guy and Alex grabbed the guy and slammed him against the wall and then took out an electricity gun and Alex electrocuted the anti-America guy really bad and he started screaming and yelling in pain and Alex was able to kill the guy. And then Alex noticed at the anti-America guy that he had a microchip and a lot of liquid soy milk coming out his cuts and Alex knew right away that something was not right. And Alex started running out of the bookstore as a lot of people in the store were shocked at just what happened. Alex then started running upstairs in the mall and he noticed some anti-America thieves wearing black outfits and wearing a lot of communist propaganda T-shirts on them. Alex saw them and he started running and he ran out of the building. Alex ran out of the mall and started running towards one of the west lake buildings and then Alex turned back and all of a sudden, a lot of motorcycles and black cars started chasing Alex, Alex then saw a Lamborghini Countach car Alex sadly had steel the car and Alex got into the car and Alex was able to steel the car, and Alex was able to get the car out of it's parking spot. And Alex turned back and he got really shocked and saw a lot of communist cars about to come at Alex and then right away Alex put his foot on the gas pedal and Alex started going fast on the road in downtown Seattle. Alex then started driving the car really fast through the streets and Alex speed through up 5 red lights. As Alex got around Pike place market, Alex then took a sharp turn and Alex kept on going really fast and more people started saying a lot of crazy things as Alex was speeding, more of the Anti-America in black cars and black motorcycles kept on chasing him "We are going to kill you Reagan lover!!!!!!" they yelled as they were driving their vehicles and going after Alex. And then they took out grenade launchers and started firing at Alex and causing a lot of explosions in the process. Alex then kept on going really fast and Alex parked the car and Alex looked his coat pocket and he was able to find a DD4 gun and Alex found the gun and Alex reloaded the gun and Alex pointed and aimed carefully and Alex started to fire 19 bullets at lot of anti-America people that were going to ram into him. And Alex was able to blow up their tires really badly and cause a really huge explosion and Alex reloaded his gun again and Alex pointed the gun at another motorcycle coming at him and Alex shot at that particular motorcycle and was able to cause another explosion.

Alex then pulled the stick shift lever on the car and Alex was able to back up the care really fast while turning his head back. And then Alex was able to put the car back on drive from reverse and Alex kept on going fast on the road and a lot more anti-America people kept on chasing after him. Alex kept on driving and Alex started heading towards Lower Queen Ann and around Seattle Center, Alex put the pedal to the medal and Alex's car started going off a lot of hills and slamming on the ground and kept on going. More anti-America kept on shooting at Alex and Alex started drifting the car left and right and Alex would throw a lot of bombs from behind at the bad guys. As Alex kept on driving, he sadly was out of bullets in DD4 gun and Alex knew he really needed to use a weapon and fast. Finally, Alex while he was driving remembered that his watch could fire lasers even from far distances. Alex was able to take off his watch and Alex aimed his spy watch as more anti-America were on his tail, as they took out more guns and more weaponry, Alex pressed the sliver button and Alex started firing 12 lasers at the thugs chasing him, Alex while he was driving was able to blow up a lot of black cars and motorcycles that were chasing after him and Alex kept on going really fast on the road, he noticed that he was in Ballard and was on the Ballard bridge and Alex kept on going really fast and then Alex was able to take sharp right turn and more of the thugs kept on chasing him. Alex then turned the car around and then Alex started going really fast and then the car started heading towards a ledge that was towards the water. As Alex flew off the ledge in the car, Alex jumped out of the car and Alex was falling in the air and Alex fell into the water in Ballard. Alex was able to swim back to the surface and he started swimming to the ledge and he was able to climb up the docks and he around where the boats, Alex then hid behind a wall and he was soaking wet and he smelled really bad, and more anti-America people showed up and they had guns and riffles in their hands. Alex then noticed some of them walking towards him and Alex hid behind a crate and Alex was able to grab him from behind and punch him in the face knock him out and Alex was able to steel his riffle gun and then a lot of anti-

American thugs in anti-America cars showed up and then they took out a lot of riffle guns and they started shooting at Alex. And then Alex hid behind a wall and Alex loaded his gun and he started shooting around 44 bullets at the thugs and Alex was able to kill around 8 different thugs and then the thugs that were alive, kept on shooting bullets at Alex and Alex kept on running and more explosions kept having and some of the Ballard port dock started catching on fire. And then all of a sudden, one of the anti-America people took out a rocket launcher and blasted a lot of rockets at Alex. And Alex did a lot of summersaults and did a lot of backflips and front flips and landed on his feet and Alex took out his spy watch and firing at a lot more anti-America people and caused more explosions and the Ballard port building started catching on fire. And Alex kept on running and Alex took out the riffle gun and he started shooting 99 bullets and also kept on reloading as well. And then another anti-America person tried to punch Alex in the face, but Alex dodged the punch and kicked the thug in the balls and punched him in the face and threw in the harbor.

And then at the same time, Alex was in Ballard, Sadie and Spencer was in their car and they saw the fire and were shocked "Spencer what's going on over there?" Sadie asked, "I don't know" Spencer said but then they just kept on driving.

Alex meanwhile, kept on running and he kept on shooting at more thugs that were coming at him like crazy. Along with one of the port buildings that caught on fire. As Alex kept on running, Alex then started running on the street and he started running to Ballard. Alex was also able to find a pathway that led to the admiral house by the dock and Alex sneaked on to the property and was able to loose the anti- America thugs that were chasing him. And then Alex went into the house and he was able to see the view of downtown Seattle and also the buildings and the space needle as well. And then Alex went back into the house and he started looking around the house and none of the staff of the place haven't come back yet. And then Alex turned on the TV and he was able to see a commercial that Sadie and Spencer did and found out that a local meet up with them was in Ballard. But Alex didn't think very much of it. And also around the same time, Alex was around the Admiral house, Sadie and Spencer then drove around the Ballard port dock fire. And also since Spencer had military and former police experience he saw the sight and got out of his car. "What happen over here?" He asked "A lot of pro USSR and pro communist people attacked a normal guy in a suit and tie" the police officer said "oh dear that's terrible" Spencer said "is he alright at least?" Spencer asked "We have no idea where he might have gone" the officer said

And then after that social conversation, Spencer then went back into his car and him and Sadie started driving to Ballard. And at this point, it's very important to know that Sadie and Spencer own a nightclub and bar called the ruby league. Now you may say why it's called that but the real reason is because the city of Ballard in Seattle is home to a lot of strange and crazy people. As Alex was still at the admiral house, Alex then lie down on the bed and then fell asleep and then one of the staff saw him and they grabbed Alex and they took to a van and put him inside the trunk.

And the van itself just so happens to be going to the Ruby league. And then as Alex was asleep, the two staff members then picked up Alex from both his feet and his head and then they went inside and they threw Alex on a coach while he was sleeping. And at first the club and bar was a very quiet and not a lot of people and Alex was able to sleep peacefully. But then around 4PM or so, Alex started hearing some noise and he slowly started to realize he was in a very strange place, and Alex looked around he saw people in the bar drinking, pool tables, and people playing a lot of interesting looking games, people playing arcade games and watching TV games. Alex got off the couch and Alex looked around and there were posters of Sadie everywhere and then Alex kept on walking and Alex then saw a person wearing A Sadie shirt that looked like he was a fan of her work. And Alex reluctantly sat by him and then same gentlemen as he was drinking his beer then turned to Alex "Are you here to Sadie as well?" he asked "I don't think so, I don't even know how the hell I got here, I have been sleeping for 3 hours or so" Alex said and then little did Alex know, he was sitting on a trap door and then all of a sudden, the trap door opened and then Alex fell through the trap door and the chair he was sitting on dumbed Alex on to a moving slide and Alex started going really fast on the slide and Alex had a concerned look on his face as he was sliding faster "Hello welcome to the Ruby league, you have been chosen to be in my special nightclub, and you stepped on the VIP chair and have been chosen to me in person. And you have entered into the girl made house. Wahooooooo" Sadie's voice said, as she was super excited to meet Alex. And then Alex kept sliding down the slide and saw a lot of clips of Sadie talking to many of her guests on her talk show and seeing a lot of people dancing in lights. "What in the hell am I watching?" Alex thought inside of his head.

And then all of a sudden, Alex fell off the slide and he landed on to a sofa and felt the force very rapidly and then Sadie started doing a girly laugh. "Welcome" Sadie said and then Sadie laughed again "Welcome to my crazy night club Alex Aussmen" Sadie said and then the lights turned on Sadie showed up as she walked out of another moving object and Sadie showed up in a very beautiful and very gorgeous and very stunning 1980's dress that was purple and she was wearing pink high heels and wearing 1980s sunglasses "I have herd so much about you Mr. Aussmen" Sadie said "Like what kind of things?" Alex asked "Well a lot of good things. Such as from reading my viewer chart that you watch my show and have been doing so since the early 80's. And you also like very beautiful women as well" Sadie said "Oh okay that's actually very accurate" Alex said "And I have read your reports that you are like the best secret agent in the Seattle area as well" Sadie said "And you are finally here in my sight and it's a huge pleasure to meet you as well" Sadie said and then all of a sudden, Sadie got very very close to Alex and she put both of her hands on Alex's face like she was going to kiss him on the lips and Sadie right away was fascinated with Alex's good looks and how handsome he was. "Well I really love your energy and how free spirited you are. But I think I might already have a girl I like" Alex said "Hmmmm oh what's the matter Alex..." Sadie said and then all of a sudden Sadie started bending down and showing her cleavage to Alex to get more of his attention and then all of a sudden, Spencer came in the room, "I don't your funny tricks won't work Sadie, I'll see what I can do" Spencer said and then Spencer was wearing a white suit and tie with 1980's sunglasses and Sadie walked back to Spencer "Good evening Mr. Aussmen, I'm Spencer, and Yeah my girlfriend Sadie loves to hit on guys all the time just to really get into your head" Spencer said "Yeah I can really see that" Alex said "Anyway reason we choice you on the trap door spotlight chair is because we may not be staying in Seattle for very long and planning to move our headquarters back to Minnesota and won't be on the Seattle channels anymore, and since things are getting full, we would be honored if you came with us and be our bodyguard in Minnesota?" Spencer asked as Alex herd the sentence and the question, he then had a lot of thoughts going through his head and the question sounded very crazy as well "Look it was very nice to meet you and Sadie but I'm already employed by Seattle Agencies and I can't leave that agency I'm sorry" Alex said "Oh come on Alex, if you work for us, you will get paid double at what your working currently, also Sadie and I saw video tape of you taking out the Sandinistas in Nicaragua as well and also back in 1976 as well, And if you come with us, I will show a lot of different women as well, and then you will also see more of the world as well" Spencer "But I can't just leave however my current job, also I am not made out of money and..." Alex said but then Alex was interrupted as Spencer pulled out a check for 400 million dollars, "Is that 400 million dollars?" Alex asked, "It is Mr. Aussmen this would be money that would double everything, not just that but I can set you up with a lot of stocks as well and have multiple sources of income other then being a secret agent" Spencer said "also you don't need to move anywhere, you can still live in Seattle, but just be with us for a while. What's it going to be Alex?" Spencer said Alex then started thinking about it for a couple of minutes and then he was able to come up with a choice "Alright, I will go and be you guys new bodyguard" Alex said and then Sadie got really excited and she started hugging Alex "Thank you, thank you, thank you, you will not regret this one bet" Sadie said "Oh your going to have so much fun Alex" Sadie said

And then during that same night, Alex started drinking a lot of beer with Sadie and Spencer and eating food with them as well. And as they kept on talking, Alex really enjoyed their company as well and love their personalities and Sadie and Spencer got to know more about Alex as well. And then as Alex was laughing and having fun with Spencer and Sadie, there was a robotic dog with robot eyes that started spying on Alex and the transmission was going to a submarine in the ocean around where Forks, Washington is. And then Victoria Borodina started looking the TV of Alex laughing with Sadie and Spencer "Go to Minnesota Alex, but even if you go to Minnesota, your evil granny Victoria is going haunt your thoughts and I will send more communist soldiers into the USA and go and capture you and kidnap my little prince Alex and my evil plan will be so harmful that you won't be able to stop me. And prepare to bomb the United States and the USA will be no more....MUAHAHAHAHAHAHAHAHAHAHAHAHAHAHAHAHAHAHAHAHAHAHA HA HEHEHEHEHEHEHEHEHEHEHEHEHEHEHEHEHEHEHEHEHEHEHEHEHEHEHE HEHEHEHEHEHEHEHEHEHEHEHEHEHEHEHEHEHEHEHEHEHEHEHEHEHEHE HEHEHEHEHEHEHEEHEHEHEHEHEHEHEHEHE" Victoria laughed as her laugh was sounding more and more like an evil witch and even though Alex was excited to go on a new adventure of sorts, he knew that there was a lot of evil waiting for him.

Chapter 2, Meeting Sadie and Spencer's bodyguard in Minnesota

Alex kept on hanging out with Spencer and Sadie under the nightclub and they all had really wonderful conversations as well that night. And then around 11PM or so, Alex then was able to call a taxi and the taxi was able to take him back to his apartment in downtown Seattle and then as he got there, Alex started packing a lot of clothes in his huge bag including a lot of suits and other clothes and bathing suits as well. And then Alex took a shower and then he shaved some of his left over facial hair that was on his face and then he took off his clothes and then he went to sleep and then he was able to set an alarm to wake up around 4AM. And as Alex was sleeping, he really didn't know what to expect when being Sadie and Spencer's bodyguards but he knew doing this was a trip of a lifetime that was somewhat a break from his usual secret agent missions that he did in the past. And then he was also thinking about Jenny as well and while he was sleeping, he started developing a lot of sexual feelings for her and he often would get erections that would last for 9 hours as well. As Alex's alarm started to ring and go off like crazy, Alex then got up and he was able to take a shower, get dressed and he was able to put on a 1980's suit and tie and also put a par of 1980's sunglasses on his head as well. Alex was able to go out the door with his bag and his other important items as well. Alex then was able to call a taxi through a pay phone and in 30 minutes or so, the taxi arrived and Alex went into the cab and the cab started driving to Sea-Tac airport. And Alex knew that this one of his top secret missions that he was going on and also he didn't have enough time to tell Michael and Tony that he was leaving and going to be out of town and knew that this was going to be a long trip.

The car was able to get to Sea-Tac airport and the car was able to drop off Alex around the gate, "Glad you can make it Alex" Sadie said and then as Alex got out of the car, Sadie was so happy, that she ran up to Alex was able to give him a really hug that lasted for 20 minutes or so and Sadie just loved touching Alex especially his backside and touching hit buttocks as well. And then all of a sudden, Sadie released him "So are you ready to go to the mid-west?" she asked "Oh I am ready, also another thing to point out is that I have been to mid-west back I believe in 1985 or so when I went on a mission in Chicago and stopping a crazy highway from being built" Alex said "Oh okay, sounds like you know where your things are, that's great" Sadie said "And also that's really amazing Alex" Sadie also said "Oh thank you" Alex said "Well we better get going otherwise we are going to miss our flight" Spencer said "Oh yeah I agree man" Alex said and then Alex, Spencer, and Sadie started heading to the ticket counter and they were able to get their tickets and then from there, they also went through customs well and Alex was able to use a special gadget so that the metal detectors wouldn't get triggered. As they all got to the terminal and got to their gate number and just sat down in the chairs. As Alex was sitting down, he then went to go get a Wendy's cheeseburger and fries and lemonade and also get himself a frosty as well and then as he came back to his seats Spencer turned his head and saw Alex eating "yo man that's a lot of food, do you always use a lot?" Spencer asked "Oh yeah I always do my man, mainly because I'm always on the move and walking and running and always have energy and never get tired" Alex said "you must have a very hard time sleeping I assume" Spencer said "Not really, I always drink milk before I go to bed or a milkshake" Alex said "How many calories do you end up burning?" Spencer asked "Somewhere around 5,000 maybe" Alex said "Oh that's really amazing Alex" Sadie said "Yeah your like the terminator my man" Spencer said And then after one hour later, Alex, Sadie, And Spencer then herd the announcement in the airport and that their plane to Minnesota was about to take off and boarding was about to begin. And so they all started getting up on their feet and they started heading in line. And then as they got in line, they then sat around the middle part of the plane and Alex got to sit in the aisle seat. And from there, the airplane started taking off from Seattle, Washington to St. Paul, Minnesota and on the plane, Alex was sleeping on the plane and Alex was dreaming a lot about Jenny and having crazy dreams where Alex was making out with her on the beach and they were in very sexy swimsuits as well. And then as Alex was sleeping, Sadie and Spencer were able to get their food on the airplane and then Alex would get up around certain times during the plane ride and also drink like a coke or a ginger ale as well.

And then after a couple hours, the airplane landed and landed in the airport, and then everybody in the plane then I started getting off the airplane. And then Alex, Spencer, Sadie got off the airplane, Alex was really looking around with his eyes because he staring at the elements in the airport. Especially at the culture elements. And then they all started heading to baggage clam and went to get their suitcases and then they started heading to a rent a car on one of the buses. And then as they got to the rent a car place, they then got to the place, the three of them got in lane and then they all started waiting. "So what kind of car do you guys want?" Alex asked "you know that's a really good question Alex, I think we really need a car that is really good when it comes to travel" Sadie said "Like a RV or motorhome or a trailer?" Alex asked, "Yeah something like but a little small" Sadie said "Sounds good. If you actually want to know a story, My best friend Michael and I actually drove in one when were heading to Dallas, Texas on a mission" Alex said "That must have been really fun, and Texas is a very beautiful state" Sadie said "It is" Alex said "What kind of mission was it?" Sadie asked "Well it was a mission where we with a French painter and he was selling art at an art convention" Alex said "oh wow" Sadie said "Oh yeah" Alex said and then as the line kept on moving, the three of them were able to get the front of the line. "Can I help you people?" the rent a car person asked "Yeah we really need a traveling car?" Sadie asked "Alright I think we have the car for you sweetie" the rent a car person said and then all of a sudden, they then went outside and they saw a van that looked like a hippie van but it was more modern looking as well "This car is a good mix between car and a motor-home" the rent a car person said "Oh sweet that's really wonderful, we will take it" Sadie said "And also the car rent is around 300$" the person pointed out "Alright that's pretty cheap" Spencer said and then as they got the car, Spencer and Sadie started packing their things in the car, and then so did Alex as well. And then as they all got into the car, Alex went to the back seat and he started looking around and he right away started getting flash backs to 1978. "So who is driving?" Alex asked "why don't you drive and give it a go" Spencer said and then Spencer threw the keys to Alex and Alex was able to catch the keys. And then Alex climbed into the driver's seat and he put the keys into the main car hole and then Alex then started turning on the car and right away, Alex started driving the car and Alex started to drive on a highway and he was driving on the highway and heading to downtown St. Paul and Alex saw a lot of the different buildings and then Alex saw the mall of America and Alex started driving there "I would imagine you guys need some champing gear cause of your traveling stuff right?" Alex asked "Yeah defiantly for sure Alex" Sadie said "And then also some cameras as well" Spencer said "Sounds good" Alex said and then Alex started driving to mall of America.

And then as they got there, Sadie and Spencer started going into stores and they started getting a lot of different 1980's camping gear, and then Alex was with them and he also looked around and looking at the different clothes that were there. And then Sadie would come out of the dressing room "Alex how does this look on me?" Sadie asked "I love it Sadie, it looks very beautiful and very stunning on you" Alex said "oh thank you" and then in another store, Spencer was looking at different cameras that were both video and normal cameras as well. And Spencer was able to buy them with new sweat what so ever. And then as everyone was done shopping, they then started heading to the car and Alex got into the driver's seat "So where are we going next?" Alex asked "We are going to my house that is in one of the suburb neighborhoods" Sadie said "Sweet" Alex said and then all of a sudden, Sadie was able to hand Alex was directions and Alex started driving and fallowing the directions to get to Sadie's house. And then as Alex kept on driving, he then turned his head to the left and he saw a normal looking 2-story house that had a normal backyard and the style of the house looked very castle like and then Alex stood in his tracks and he just starred at the house in amazement "So this is your home?" Alex asked "Oh yeah this is where Spencer and I live and also April lives here as well" Sadie said, "That's really cool" Alex said "you have to see more things, it does a lot of other cool stuff, especially underground" Sadie said And then Alex was able to park the car, and then they all got unloaded the car with all the things that Sadie and Spencer bought and they started heading into the castle house.

As they all got into the house, Inside of the house was really fancy and there was a lot of paintings and art everywhere, a TV room, and then a really fancy looking kitchen and then also there was bedrooms around the other side of the room as well. "Man guys, this house is amazing and really incredible" Alex said "Oh thank you Alex, this is a house that is been in my family for a lot of generations and it was built by my ancestors that came from England and also from France as well" Sadie said "Oh that's really amazing" Alex said "What about your parents?" Alex asked, "Well my mom and dad were also really wealthy and you know he didn't really have a big time job, but he just always invested in the stock market a lot, and then that's what April and I and Spencer did as well" Sadie said "That's actually really smart, That's something I really need to do, cause I know that I can't be a secret agent forever" Alex said "Well how much do you make Alex?" Spencer asked "Well so far around 400,000$ a year but it use to be a lot less when I was a teenager" Alex said, "I see" Spencer said "But yeah if you stick with us Alex, we will teach you how to make a lot of money" Spencer said "Thanks Spencer" Alex said "But you also have to see underground part of the house as well" Sadie said And then Alex, Sadie, And Spencer then started walking downstairs and then Sadie pressed a button and then parts of the wall started to open up and they all went into the elevator and then all of a sudden, the elevator started going down. And then as the elevator stopped, they all got out of the elevator and Alex was really amazed and around the basement and underground parts, there was a swimming pool, hot-tub, a lot of arcade games, and then also some darts. And then also a basketball court and other forms of entertainment. And then there was also a gym down there as well. "Oh wow this is amazing" Alex said "Yeah this were we all come down and play and chill down here as well" Sadie said "And then we also even fire pit as well to cock marshmallows" Spencer said "This place is like my apartment on steroids" Alex said "So Alex buddy, what do you want to do first?" Spencer asked "I don't know, I'm going to try out the game room" Alex said and then all of a sudden, Alex then started trying out the game room and then after a couple of hours, Alex and Spencer then played each other in one on one basketball. And then after doing that, Alex, Sadie, and Spencer had some food as well and they were all having Hot dogs with cheddar cheese on them along with relish and onions and they also had popcorn with butter on them as well "Well I must say you guys, thank you so much for letting me come with you guys, and your house is incredible" Alex said "oh thank you Alex" Sadie said "So what is planned for tomorrow? if you don't mind me asking." Alex asked, "Well, we are going to do another show in downtown Minnesota. You don't really have much to do, you just are bodyguard and you wear a suit and make sure nothing happens to Spencer and I. And then we also get ready to travel again" Sadie said "Sounds really good, I can't wait" Alex said

And then during that night, Alex then went to sleep and as Alex was sleeping, he heard a lot of noises and also the snow that was falling down on the ground. And then the next morning, Alex then woke up and he then took a shower and then he also got dressed into normal 1980's style clothing and then before Sadie and Spencer got up, Alex then started looking around the house. And Alex even looked at the window and he saw the snow falling down and then all of a sudden, Alex herd one of the doors in the house open and it was Spencer and Sadie walking towards him "Morning Alex" Sadie said "Morning Sadie" Alex said "How did you sleep?" Spencer asked him "I slept really well. What about you?" Alex asked "really good, yeah in this house, you will always get a nights rest" Spencer said "That's awesome my man" Alex said "Well I better make us some breakfast and we have a big show to do" Spencer said and then during that morning, Alex, Sadie, and Spencer all started eating breakfast and then after breakfast, everyone started getting dressed and then Alex got on a suit and tie and he was able to brush his teeth. And then Alex got into Sadie's car and he was able to drive Sadie and Spencer to downtown Minnesota and started driving to their studio. And as Alex kept on driving, he was really amazed at how big everything was, and then Alex drove into the parking garage and he was able to park the car. And then as Alex was able to park the car, Sadie, Alex, and Spencer started heading to the elevator and the elevator started going up and they were going to the 60th floor. And then as they got to the floor, Alex then saw a lot of directions and posters of Sadie and Spencer and Alex fallowed them to their dressing room and then Sadie stopped and turned around "Alright what you do is just check for tickets and that's all you do." Sadie said, "Alright sweet, shouldn't be that hard I don't think" Alex said "good luck and be careful Alex" Sadie said and then all of a sudden, Alex then started walking out of the stage and he was guarding the main stage and checking for tickets from the people coming in. And for the most part, Alex was able to do this really well, and also just incase there was a bad person that was coming in, he also had a pistol gun in his suit pocket. But then as Alex ticketing people, there all of a sudden, was another beautiful and a very gorgeous and very stunning girl with blonde hair and she also eyes that were a mix between green and blue eyes, and she walking in there with her mom as well, Alex wasn't really paying attention anybody that was coming and was just mainly doing the job he was tasked to do. And then the same girl with those same features, just smiled at him and just said "Thank you"

And then as the show was going to start and everybody start getting in their seats and as the lights got shut off, there was a lot of lights that were flashing and then the song "Papa don't preach by Madonna" and then Spencer did the announcing work "Live from Minnesota in front of a live studio audience it is the Living With Adventures with Sadie. And now without further a do, here is Sadie Holbrock" Spencer said on the microphone and then all of a sudden, a lot of the crowd started clapping and really going crazy and also screaming with excitement as well. And then all of a sudden, the curtain opened and Sadie was in a very beautiful pink 1980's style dress as well. "Thank you, thank you, thank you everyone, my name is Sadie Holbrock and I do this show every week, and if your someone that really loves to travel and see the world, well this show is for you" Sadie said with a smile on her face.

And then as Alex was behind the door, little did Alex knew there was a lot of evil looking people that had scares and ugly finger nails that were starting to come towards Alex while he was guarding, then one of the guards ended up punching Alex in the face and Alex ended up being knocked out, and then Alex fell to the ground, and then the thugs grabbed Alex and they put him inside a bag and they started taking to the top parts of the building and around a basement. And then after a couple of hours into the show and around some of the breaks in between, Sadie noticed that Alex was gone and she really started getting concerned for him. "Oh my god Spencer Alex is gone" Sadie said, "Do you know where he might be?" She asked "Sadly I don't know. And yeah I noticed that he is gone as well. And I think some shady looking people kidnapped him and they didn't look very nice either" Spencer said "I'm going to go look for him Sadie" Spencer said and then Spencer then went out of the studio and he had a gun in his coat and he started looking around the building for Alex.

And then all of a sudden in the abandon room of the skyscraper in Minnesota, the bag was lifted from Alex's head and Alex had duck tape on his mouth and his hands were tied up and in duck tape as well. And then Alex started hearing a very evil, very creepy, and a very evil witch laugh coming towards "HEHEHEHEHEHEHEHE HEHEHEHEHEHEHEHEHEHE!!!!!!!! Good evening Mr. Aussmen!!!!!!! And hello, hello, hello my handsome little boy!!!!!!" the witch voice said and then all of a sudden, it turned out the evil Victoria Borodina and Alex for the first time saw her new look. And Alex started grunting in anger and he was trying to get free "I have right where I want you Alex, and you nowhere to run and even though you are in Minnesota, I was always going to be around to make your life a living hell. And also I am a lot more uglier and more witch like because I have had more plastic surgery done on me and now I look like an evil witch from all the scary stories, and if you really thought my Social justice Warrior and colored hair was scary, I think my new look will give you a lot of nightmares Alex" Victoria said "And then I also have these yellow zits on me as well Mr. Aussmen!!!!!!" Victoria also added and then she did another soft and evil witch laugh. And then Alex kept on grunting and trying to get free "Do you even know why I am in Minnesota to begin with Mr. Aussmen?" Victoria asked "It's mostly because your friend Sadie Holbrock's ancestors stole a lot of money and gold and treasure from my ancestors and I tend to kill her and her sister and her boyfriend to have it back and this time you will not stand in my way little boy" Victoria said "Put him outside to freeze to death" Victoria said to her thugs "With pleasure boss" one of her thugs said and then all of a sudden, Victoria's thugs grabbed Alex and they started going upstairs and they took the elevator to the top of the skyscraper building. And then the thugs started tying up Alex and they even ripped the duck tape off of his mouth and Alex was in a lot of pain.

And after Sadie's show was all done, then all of a sudden, there was a lot of shooting that happened and a lot of people were screaming and people were really scarred. And then all of a sudden, Sadie also got really scarred and then all of a sudden, Victoria and her thugs showed up into the room "Good Evening Ms. Holbrock" Victoria said "Who are you?..." Sadie said in a very scarred voice "Oh I'm someone that really knows your family history really well and I do believe you have money that belongs to me" Victoria said "And if you don't give it me, I will kill or kidnap someone in this room or someone that did go to your show" Victoria said in a very evil witch like voice and then all of a sudden, Victoria and her thugs started getting really close to Sadie and Sadie started getting really scared and all of a sudden, they grabbed Sadie and they tied her up somewhere on the stage. And some of her thugs tried to get one of the 1980's computers that was around the backstage on the studio and they started hacking into her bank account and they were able to put all of Sadie's money into a keycard.

Meanwhile at the same time, Spencer found Alex as he was tied up and he un-tied him on the roof and the snow was coming down on him like crazy. Spencer then had some hot water in his bottle and dumped some hot water on Alex to warm him up. Alex's body got trigged and warmed up and Alex was able to get back on his feet. "Are you okay Alex?" Spencer said "Yeah I think so buddy, we have to stop Borodina and her thugs cause I know she is up to something. Come on!!!!!" Alex said and then all of a sudden, Alex and spencer started running down the stairs and going at a rapid pace. And then as they got to the main floor, they saw a lot more thugs and they had deadly hand guns in their hand, and then all of a sudden, they started shooting around 77 bullets at Alex and Spencer, Alex and Spencer were able to avoid the bullets and were able to take cover. Alex then reloaded his Walter gun and Alex pointed his gun and grabbed his gun with two hands and Alex started firing 99 bullets and Alex was able to shoot around 9 thugs coming at him and was able to shoot them in the head and kill them. And then all of a sudden, more thugs started coming at them and they had A33 riffles in their hand and they started shooting around 900 bullets at Alex and Spencer and they able to take cover. "I got these guys, go save Sadie, go Alex!!!!" Spencer said and then all of a sudden with all the speed in his strange and weird body, Alex then started running to the show room for dear life, and then as more thugs were shooting at Alex, Alex then dived on the floor and then Alex was sliding on the floor and then as Alex was sliding on the floor, Alex then kicked one of the thugs in the legs and then Alex was able to use both of his legs and grab and slam to the ground head first. And then a lot of thugs that didn't have any weapons started coming towards him and they started throwing a lot of punches and kicks at Alex. And then Alex was able to dodge the attacks and throw some punches and kicks back at 4 different thugs that were coming at him.

And then Alex was able to punch one of the thugs in the face and also grab another one by the arm and slam against the wall. And then Alex was able to kick another in the face and then kick another one in the stomach and knock that one out as well. And then Alex kept on fighting more thugs and then Alex was able to punch 3 more of them in the face and then Alex grabbed a fire department axe and stabbed 4 more of them in the stomach and kill them. And then after killing the thugs, Alex then kept on running and Alex breaked the door open and Victoria was on stage and more thugs were pointing their riffle guns at Alex and Victoria had the keycard in her left hand and showed it to Alex "Looking for this!!!...." Victoria said and then Victoria was pointing a gun at Sadie "you are very too late Mr. Aussmen, I have already gotten most of Sadie's money and in a couple of minutes I will use her money to build more weapons from my castle in Ukraine and then I will rule the world and destroy everyone that stands in my way" Victoria said "You will never get away with this Borodina!!!!!!!" Alex said "Oh I think I have already have little boy!!!!, and now the time has come for me to escape in my helicopter" Victoria said in her evil witch voice "it ain't going to happen you ugly Ukraine bitch!!!!!" Alex said in anger in his voice and then without Alex knowing, Sadie was able to get herself free and then all of a sudden, Sadie was able to kick Victoria in the face and punch her in the face and knock the keycard out of her hand. "Alex grab the card!!!!" Sadie said and then Alex started running and all of Borodina's thugs started shooting a lot of bullets at Alex and then Alex reloaded his gun and then Alex started shooting at the thugs and Alex was able to fire around 15 bullets and Alex was able to kill around 5 thugs that were shooting at him and then Alex reloaded his gun and more thugs were shooting at him and then Alex started shooting 20 more bullets out of his gun and then Alex started running and he jumped on stage and Alex kept on shooting at the thugs coming at him and Alex was able to kill 40 thugs that were coming at him and shoot them in the head and then also shoot them in one of the eyes. And then Alex finally was able to get to Sadie and un-tie her "Thank you Alex" Sadie said "Your welcome Sadie" Alex said "Go find Spencer and find a safe place and get out of here" Alex said "Alright okay" Sadie said "Alex be careful they have a lot of guns and a lot of Ukraine thugs as well that hate America" Sadie said "Don't worry I'm going to be okay. Trust me" Alex said and then Sadie started running out of the skyscraper and she went into one of the elevator with Spencer "Where's Alex?" Spencer asked, "He is going after the thugs" Spencer said "Man that guy has a lot of fight in him" Spencer said

And then as Alex was in the room, one of Borodina's thugs threw a bomb at Alex and there was a huge explosion and all of a sudden, the building started catching on fire and then Alex did a summer-sault and then all of a sudden Alex saw the same girl with blonde hair that said thank you and the girl was looking at Alex and the girl was looking for her mom who was trapped in the building. And then all of a sudden Borodina grabbed the girl with blonde hair and she started getting really scarred and Borodina grabbed her by the wrist and then she took out a pistol gun and pointed the gun at her "Somebody help me, someone help me!!!!" she cried "Shut up you stupid American girl!!!!!" Borodina yelled and then Borodina threaten her with a taser. And then Alex was able to catch up with Borodina and Alex had a Walter gun in his right hand "If you fallow me the girl dies!!!!!!" Borodina yelled and then the girl started screaming as she was really scarred and then Alex saw a window and then Alex broke one of the windows and Alex jumped out the window and then Alex started sky diving and falling and then Alex pressed a button his spy watch and then all of a sudden, Alex had wings come out of his fancy shoes and then Alex started gliding in the air and then Alex saw Borodina in a blue and yellow limo. And then on the ground, Borodina forced the girl with blonde hair to get into the limo and then the car started driving really fast. And then moments later, Alex then landed on the ground and Alex started looking around and then he saw a motorcycle and Alex was able to steel the motorcycle and then Alex started up the motorcycle and then Alex all of a sudden, started going really fast and he started going around 200 miles per hour on the bike.

And then as the limo started going really fast on the road in snowy Minnesota, Alex then started going really fast on the motorcycle and he was speeding through a lot of cars and speeding a lot of red lights as well. And Alex was wearing special sunglasses that were protecting his eyes from the snow. And then Borodina turned and saw Alex chasing her "Aussmen, Only Aussmen, Kill him!!!!!" Borodina said and then all of a sudden, her driver started pressing a lot of buttons and throwing a lot of weaponry at Alex. And then Alex was able to put on the pedal to medal and go really fast on the motorcycle and then Alex pulled out a ZMG gun and then all of a sudden, Alex started firing around 200 bullets at Borodina's limo and shooting at her window. And then Alex was able to dodge a lot of cars that were coming at him and then Alex was able to go off a lot of ramps and Alex was doing a lot of front and backflips while he was on the motorcycle while he was up in the air and then Alex was able to land on the ground and keep on going really fast. And then Borodina inside of her limo, she then pressed a lot of buttons and she fired a lot of machine gun and rockets and missiles at Alex and then Alex was able to dodge the missiles and rockets that were coming at him and then the rockets and missiles caused a lot of explosion in downtown Minnesota and some buildings started catching on fire. And then as the chase was going on, Alex saw Borodina's limo that was going towards a warehouse that had a landing roof on top of the building. And then Borodina was able to park her limo and then she got out of the limo and grabbed the girl "Get out!!!!!" She yelled and then she pointed a gun at her head "Otrymaty vertolit hotovyj!!!!" Borodina said in Ukraine and then all of her thugs started getting ready to get the helicopter ready to go. But then all of a sudden, Alex was able to get into the building and then more thugs saw him and they started shooting a lot of bullets at Alex and then Alex took out his gun and then he started firing more bullets back at Borodina's thugs and also taking cover as well. Alex then reloaded his gun and then he kept on shooting more bullets at the thugs and shooting them in the head and also in other areas as well. And then Alex kept on running he then saw Borodina taking the girl into the helicopter "let her go Borodina!!!!!" Alex said as he was pointing and aiming his gun at her "you loose again Alex!!!!" Borodina said and then all of a sudden, Borodina threw a bomb and Alex was able to dodge the bomb and all of a sudden, there was a huge explosion and the warehouse started catching on fire. And then Alex started looking around and he saw a snowboard object that was in the warehouse and Alex stepped on to the snowboard and it actually turned out to be flying board and then Alex pressed on the button and board started zooming up in the air and then Alex took his gun and he saw Borodina's helicopter and her helicopter started heading towards the mall of America stadium and then helicopter turned back and the helicopter started firing a lot of missiles and rockets at Alex. And then Alex was able to control the flying board really well and he was able to dodge all of the missiles and rockets coming at him. And then Alex was able to reload his gun and then Alex kept on shooting at the helicopter as he was in the sky and then Alex was able to do a lot more damage to the helicopter and cause some explosions as well. And then Borodina's face got really burned up really bad and then all of sudden, the girl with blonde hair then feel to the ground and she started screaming as she was falling in the sky and then all of a sudden, Alex then started diving down really fast and then with all of his might, Alex was able to catch her in his strong arms and then Alex turned his back and he saw Borodina's helicopter flying in the dark and snowy skies of Minnesota "We will meet again Mr. Aussmen" Borodina yelled as the helicopter was flying away

And then as Alex was going back to the ground on the flying board, the girl with blonde hair then snowy looked up at Alex's face and with her beautiful and sparking blue eyes that she had "Oh you rescued me. Oh you're my hero, who are you by the way?" She asked "The names Aussmen...Alex Aussmen" Alex said to her "Aussmen that is a really strange and a very un-usual last name. But anyway, thank you so much for saving me, Sadly we do need to find my mom, and I think she was in the building that evil witch lady attacked" She said "Yeah I can imagine" Alex said

"Anyway what is your name?" Alex asked her "Oh I'm Rebecca by the way" Rebecca said "Rebecca who?" Alex asked again "Rebecca Olga" Rebecca said "That's also a very strange last name as well" Alex said "Anyway I will get you back on the ground and then hopefully we will find your mom as well" Alex said "So do you know Sadie Holbrock yourself?" Rebecca asked, "Yeah I do, both her and Spencer are good people" Alex said "So are you originally from Minnesota or are you from somewhere else?" Rebecca asked, "I'm from Seattle, Washington" Alex said, "Oh wow that's really cool and really amazing, I hear that's a really amazing state to live in" Rebecca said "Oh yeah it is" Alex said

And then once Alex and Rebecca landed on the ground, Alex and Rebecca started running to a pay phone and Alex was able to call a cab from the pay phone and then the taxi was able to find them. And then as they got into the cab, they then started driving back to downtown Minnesota and started driving back to Sadie's building. And then Alex was able to pay the driver and then moments later, Spencer was able to find Rebecca's mom in the building and it turned out she was trapped in one of the rooms once Rebecca was taken by Borodina "Mom are you okay?" Rebecca said and then Rebecca started running to her mom and hugging her "Oh yeah I'm fine Rebecca, I'm just glad you are okay. Anyway thank you guys for saving my daughter. I really appreciate it a lot" Rebecca's mom said, "Oh no problem you have to give it Alex, it was him that did everything" Spencer said, "Do you have the keycard Alex?" Spencer asked, "I actually have it" Rebecca said and then all of a sudden, Rebecca handed the keycard that had a lot of Sadie's money inside of the keycard and she handed to Spencer, "I was able to jack it on that witch lady's helicopter before Alex saved me" Rebecca said "alright good girl, I will try to see if I can get this back to Sadie" Spencer said

Sadie was able to catch up to Spencer and Alex and Spencer was able to hand Sadie the key card and then Rebecca and her mom went back home and Alex headed back to Sadie's house and she was able to put the keycard into the computer and get every single dime back into bank account "Oh thank god" Sadie said "Oh wow today was just so scary and horrifying as well" Sadie also added "Yeah tell me about it, Alex who were all those people?" Spencer asked him "....Sadly those are people that are after me, their leader is Victoria Borodina who is from Ukraine and she has wanted to kill for almost 12 years ever since I was teenager, and she has her evil witch claws into every terrorist organization that is out there as well" Alex said "Sounds like she knows a crazy amount of information about you" Sadie said "Oh you have no idea" Alex said "And then not only that, but she works very closely with the Sandinistas in Nicaragua and also the soviet union as well which is also really bad" Alex said "oh my god, that reminds me of someone I interviewed on my show" Sadie said "you mean Salem?" Alex said, "How did you know?" Sadie asked "Well I remember watching one of your shows and episode where you had him on and I actually saved him when he was in Portland, Oregon and Borodina and her goons were trying to kill him" Alex said "Oh my god that is terrible" Sadie said "Yeah it just goes to show that there are a lot of bad and messed up and very evil people in this world baby girl" Alex said "So what do you think we need to do Alex?" Spencer asked, "Well for the most part, I actually really don't know Spencer. But I know Borodina did try to kidnap Rebecca and I was able to save her, and I believe I'm going to try to know her a lot more I believe" Alex said "Well sounds like a really good idea Alex. Do you want Spencer and I to come with you?" Sadie asked "Yeah sure why not" Alex said and then later that day at Sadie's castle like house, Sadie then started going through her phone book and she started looking for Rebecca's first name and her last name and then finally around 4PM, Sadie was able to find Rebecca's information and also her occupation as well. And apparently Rebecca was a freelance model and she would also be in front of people in art classes. And then the next day, Alex then took a shower and then he found a way to get a bus fare card and he went to downtown Minnesota because Spencer was able to drive him. And then as Alex got to the bus office that was there, he was able to fill in his information really well and was able to get a bus pass. And then as he got out of the office, he then took a bus to the community college that was around downtown. And Alex got off the bus and then he started looking around the campus, and then Alex saw an ad that was on a bulletin board that said, "art models needed" and then Alex looked at the piece of paper really closely and then Alex started heading to the classroom and as a lot of the students were leaving the room, the main art professor looked at Alex and he had a puzzled look on his face "can I help young man?" he asked "Sure you can sir, I saw that you needed some art models for some of your classes I believe, I was wondering if that was still open?" Alex asked and then the professor looked at him for maybe 20 seconds "Yeah it's still open, have you modeled before?" he asked " Yes I have actually back in 1976 when I was teenager and then there was also other times where I had to be naked a lot as well" Alex said "yeah you're a really handsome guy. And I can tell the girls love you and you seem very boyish as well" the professor said "How much are willing to be paid?" the professor asked him "I'm willing to work minimum wage" Alex said "Alright...perfect" he said and then all of a sudden the professor gave some Alex some papers and it was some-what like a release forum and Alex gave every sort information that he knew that was in his head. And then as Alex was filling out the paper work, he then gave the paper work back to the professor "perfect" he said "Also robes are in my office and your welcome to grab one and once you strip everything off" he said "Alright sounds good sir" Alex said and then Alex walked to the back room and then Alex started taking his clothes and his underwear intel he was butt naked and then he put one of the robes to cover his naked body, and all of a sudden very slowly he then pecked his head and all of a sudden, he saw Rebecca in the class room and Rebecca had a normal look on her face. And then Alex had a smile on his face and Alex was really excited and then as the clock strikes the start time of the class, Alex then went to the middle room and he had a huge smile on his face as he saw a lot of beautiful girls wearing a lot of 1980's clothing and then the girls smiled at him back and some even chuckled did a soft laugh and then the professor gave a lecture before the class started "Now everyone we are going to draw a naked male body, it's not a test and do your best" he said and then all of a sudden, without hesitation Alex then took off his robe and Alex was butt naked and he started doing a lot of model poses and Alex then started doing a lot of poses that he did when he was modeling in New York City when he was with Dr. Jasmine Thompson that one time. But this time was completely different because he wanted to get Rebecca's attention and get to know her. As Rebecca was drawing Alex's naked body she was softly shocked as she saw how huge Alex's pennis really was but then she then smiled and then she slowly gave Alex eye contact and she started looking at Alex with a dreamy look on her face. And then Alex kept on posing and Alex felt his pennis getting bigger and bigger the more he posed. 3 hours later, as students left the room, the professor gave his own submission of the class and as the students left, Alex then put his robe back on and the professor turned to him "Well bravo young man, I can tell you really enjoyed yourself up there and a couple of my students that were girls loved your body as well" he said "oh yeah it was nothing sir" Alex said and then all of a sudden, the professor went to his desk and he started writing a Alex for 40$. Now to put this in perspective, 40$ is not a lot of money, but Alex had some very special plans for this normal check of 40$ and Alex put the money in his wallet and he started heading to nearest bus stop that was around him.

As Alex was waiting for the bus, then 20 different college girls that were in the same art class started coming up to him and they really wanted to know more about Alex as well "we really loved your body…" one of them said and then one of them really were just laughing and chuckling "so what's your name?" one of them said again "I'm Alex…Alex Aussmen" Alex said" Alex said "well it's a pleasure to meet you Alex, and we really loved your model poses as well. And we are actually having a party at an apartment, and I was wondering if you wanted to come with us?" they asked "Um…sure why the hell not" Alex said and then Alex went with the girls and he rode with one girl that had brown hair, she had blue finger nails, and she wore a lot of 1980's make up on her as well. And also she was a white girl but Alex was just amazed how beautiful she was as she was driving and also her other gestures she would make as well. And then as the car kept on going, they then parked in the parking lot and Alex started walking with the girl with blonde hair "Oh your going to like where we are taking you Alex baby boy" she said and then they went up to the elevator and then they were around 20th floor of the building and then they got off the elevator and they started walking into the building and all of a sudden, as they walked into the room and there was around 60 beautiful girls that were in 1980's bikini underwear and wearing Victoria Secrets and other ladies underwear brands as well. And then inside of the party, they were playing Papa don't preach by Madonna and there was a lot of alcohol at this party and a lot of girls being wild and really crazy. And then Alex just smiled and he said to himself "Wow" Alex said and then all of a sudden, Alex during that party drank around 4 beers and got really wasted and then 5 girls took Alex to a huge bedroom and one of them placed him on the bed "awwwwwwe such a handsome baby boy he is, I think it's time to take his clothes off" one of them said "ah okay ladies" Alex said and then all of a sudden they started tickling Alex and they were laughing and then started stripping Alex and Alex was laughing and then the girls started off their clothes, the first one that was butt naked was an African American girl, the 2nd one was a Hispanic American girl, the 3rd and 4th ones were white girls, and then the last one was a Hawaiian looking girl that had tan skin and her breaths and her bottom were really big. And the girls kept on making out for at least 5 hours. And Alex ended up sleeping with all five the girls and then as night time came around, Alex was really tired and all five of the naked girls in bed with him were softly touching him everywhere and saying "Oh Alex hold me" one of them said and then one of them even kissed Alex on the lips and went on top of Alex as well. And then all of a sudden, Alex saw the faces of the girls and then they started laughing but then all of a sudden, as Alex was making out with girls, then Alex herd a door open and Alex took a quick peak and then Alex's eyes lit up and then some of girls that were butt naked in the room all of a sudden saw a riffle gun pointed at them and then they started shooting 900 bullets at the girls and the girls were screaming in fear and crying and tears were coming out of their eyes. And then all of a sudden, the thugs and all of a sudden Victoria Borodina went into the room and saw Alex with girls he was sleeping "I got you now little boy!!!!" she said with a witch like voice "Get down!!!!!!" Alex yelled but it was too late, Victoria and her thugs sadly shoot the girls that Alex slept and all of a sudden there was a blood in the bed and then Alex was really sad as he saw the girls dead in his bed "Oh my god!!!!" Alex said and a tear fell through one his eyes and then with tears in his eyes Alex kissed all of five of them in the back and their bottoms as well and also their neck and Alex kept on breathing really hard as tears were coming out of his eyes.

And then Alex then tried to run but then one of the thugs grabbed Alex from behind and Victoria took out a whip and Alex started grunting and trying to get free "Don't be sad Alex…this room was my personal pen house and I knew I was going to trick all those college girls to be here and then kill them once I found out you were here as well" Victoria said "you fucking monster!!!!!" Alex yelled and then all of sudden Victoria hit Alex with a whip and hit him right around his private areas and Alex felt the sting very badly "You know Alex even though your 29 years old, I will always be smarter then you and I will always be a social cancer to you as well" Borodina in a very evil witch voice and then all of a sudden without Alex knowing, Spencer and Sadie were able to track Alex down from her castle house and they slowly start getting to the pen house and then as they got there and Victoria were about to whip Alex really bad, then Sadie grunted her teeth and then she fired 6 bullets at Borodina and shoot her in the arm and in back of her skull and Borodina screamed like a witch and then some of her hair fell out and then Alex got free and then Alex then punched 4 of her thugs in the face and then kicked more of them in the stomach as well. And then Victoria tried to whip Alex more but then Alex grabbed Victoria's face and pushed and electrocuted her face badly and then Victoria screamed and then Alex while he was naked started running away with Sadie and Spencer "GET THEM!!!!" Victoria screamed and then as they kept on running and Sadie and Spencer started firing bullets at Borodina and her thugs "yo man what happen to your clothes bro?" Spencer asked "it's a very long story" Alex said and then they kept on running and more of Victoria's thugs kept on shooting at Alex, Sadie, and Spencer and then as they got to the first floor, Sadie and Spencer brought their big car and Alex hid in the back so no other people would see Alex's nudity "I can imagine the art model thing went really well for you I believe" Sadie said "oh yeah it went really well" Alex said "Good" Sadie said "And then I also saw Rebecca as well and she really loved my modeling as well" Alex said "Oh that's awesome and really wonderful Alex"

Sadie said and then all of a sudden, Spencer started driving and then Sadie started firing a lot of guns and gadgets at Victoria's thug cars that were chasing them. "And we also may take Rebecca with us because I believe they may have our information and Rebecca's information as well" Spencer said "Alright okay, we may need to meet her at a certain place here in St. Paul" Alex said "oh yeah for sure man" Spencer said Spencer then kept on driving and Sadie was able to throw around 19 mine bombs at the cars and was able to blow up them in flames and they kept on moving from there. Luckily however Sadie had Rebecca's information as well and it looked like she lived in an apartment complex place in the city. And then as they got there, they then parked the car and Alex, Sadie, and Spencer ran to Rebecca's door and Sadie knocked on the door 30 times and Alex could tell Sadie had a lot of energy in her body as well because he could tell that there was a lot of allergen in her legs and Alex saw her privates moving like crazy which in Alex's mind started turning him on but Alex stayed focused and said to himself "Sadie is Spencer's girl. Focus Alex" his mind said to him and then all of a sudden, Rebecca opened the door and Rebecca saw Alex naked "Alex you're here in my apartment, what are you doing here?" she asked "Rebecca, I don't think your safe here, sadly a lot of girls from your college were killed by an old enemy of mine from the past and her thugs and her coming here and we have to leave Minnesota right now" Alex said Rebecca looked at Alex at first with a confused look but then Rebecca also was distracted by Alex's naked body and him covering his pennis in the cold water and then Rebecca smiled and said "oh okay I will go pack, I would love to come with you" Rebecca said in a very cheerful voice and then all of a sudden, Rebecca then started packing a lot of clothes and underwear and shoes and other things as well. And then as she was done packing, Rebecca and Alex then went back into Sadie and Spencer's big car and they started driving "Don't worry Alex we are going to get you some clothes to wear" Spencer said "or we could just put him in a bag and sneak him on to the barrage clam Intel we get out of the states" Sadie said in a joking matter "Oh my god" Alex thought and then Sadie started laughing and giggling in a very girly way. But then as they got there, Spencer being a police officer in the past, was able to speculate Alex's pants size and shirt and shoe size and he was able to buy Alex some normal 1980's style of clothing. And then as he was done paying for it, Alex then started putting on the clothes and in the end, Alex was wearing blue jeans, normal American tennis shoes, a normal green T shirt and a gray winter coat as well. Alex sadly didn't have any ID with him or his money because of what happened at the pen house with a lot of the college girls, but without telling Alex, Spencer was able to create a new bank account for Alex put around 800,000$ in there as well, and it was from a special world wide bank that would be used in almost every country in the world. And Spencer did all this with his computer and college knowledge as well.

And then moments later, Alex, Rebecca, Sadie and Spencer then after creating Alex's bank account, they then started to the St. Paul airport and they checked in through customs really well. And then after that, they then they got to their first gate and then they all started "So where are we going Sadie?" Rebecca asked "I don't know I think we might be going to Greece I believe mainly just because of the beaches" Sadie said with a very beautiful smile on her face "Oh I really love the sound of that baby girl" Spencer said and then Spencer and Sadie kissed each other on the lips and then as Alex was with them, Rebecca then smiled at Alex "Oh I can't wait to go to Greece with you Alex" Rebecca said "I will really enjoy being on the beach with you" Rebecca said "Yeah me too" Alex said And then as boarding began, they all sat in the middle part of the airplane and through the plane ride, Alex would drink around 6 ginger ales and then he fell asleep in the chair he was sitting on the plane. Rebecca was also sitting with him and she laid her head on Alex's right shoulder and then Rebecca started doing a lot of feminine moans. But the plane ride itself was not all fun and games and Alex thinking about Rebecca romantically, sometimes he had dreams in his head about Victoria Borodina and really hoped that she wouldn't find a way to kidnap Alex and also Sadie as well.

Chapter 3 the trip to Greece

As the airplane landed in Greece, Alex then woke up and so did other people on the plane including Sadie and Spencer. And everybody on the airplane was able to get off just fine. And then everybody including Alex went through customs and immigration very well and Alex was able to show the main person his passport and the customs person was able to stamp Alex's passport and see his papers that he filled out on the plane as well. They then went to baggage clam and right now Alex kept turning his head left and right and staring a lot of people that were speaking Greek and just observing their culture and certain mannerisms as well. And then as everybody got their bags, Sadie was able to call a taxi and they then started going to a hotel that was very normal looking. And then as they checked in, they all started exploring the country and going everywhere. Alex was wearing normal 1980's American clothing and having 1980's sunglasses on his head and Rebecca was also wearing short shorts and sandals as well. Around this point as they were traveling, Alex also noticed a very tan looking person with black hair also in Greece and he was a normal suit and tie and it looked like he was heading to a meeting somewhere.

Later that night, Alex was having a drink in the hotel lobby and Sadie and Spencer were talking about the country and Greece was really beautiful and Rebecca was drinking a martini drink as well and then all of a sudden, the same person that Alex walked by turned out to be Salem Jadon and he was meeting with the ambassador of Greece as well and Salem approached Alex very quietly and he tapped Alex on the shoulder and then Alex turned around "Hey Alex" Salem said "Salem hey buddy, what's up? How are you doing? What are you doing in Greece?" Alex asked "well the reason I'm here is because I'm here for another meeting with the Greece Ambassador and so far I think you're the only American on this trip that I have ran into" Salem said "Oh and I can also see your with some friends" Salem said "Yeah this Sadie and Spencer and Rebecca" Alex said then Sadie and Spencer introduced themselves to Salem and then Salem started drinking a Greek alcoholic drink and joining Alex as he was with Sadie, Spencer and Rebecca "So how have you been Alex?" Salem asked, "Good I think. Unfortunately in Minnesota I sadly ran into Borodina again and she sadly killed a lot of college girls as well" Alex said "dude that's terrible Alex. I'm sorry buddy" Salem said "Anyway that's one of the reasons I came to you is because I think Borodina's people might be in Greece and I think they may try to steel money from Greece government and something really fishy is going on" Salem said "Oh shit!!!! Well I will keep my eyes open Salem" Alex said and then during that night, Alex was then in his hotel room and he started looking at the window at the islands that were in Greece and he really wanted to check them out for himself. And then Alex climbed back into bed and he put his arms around Rebecca and started kissing her on the back and on the shoulders as well.

As the trip around Greece kept on going, Alex and everyone else really started exploring the country and going through many different places and saw all of the big time tourist destinations and Sadie was able to take pictures on her camera and then the coming days they then went to more places and explored more the country and Alex was really enjoyed a lot of Greek food as well. And then finally after traveling and exploring, Alex and Rebecca and Sadie then saw a nude beach and they all started taking off their clothes and they all laid in the sun butt naked and they then started putting sunscreen all over their bodies as well and sun tan oil as well. And then Rebecca and Alex started making out on a towel and smooching each other on the lips and then moments later then they ran and jumped in the ocean. But as they did so, there were a couple of strange looking people that didn't look like they were Greece that fallowed them. Alex and Rebecca swam underwater and they saw more of the ocean and the fishes and since both of them were both butt naked, they felt completely invisible to fish and other big sea-life in the ocean. And then as they were in the water, Alex and Rebecca started making out underwater and they started rising back to the surface and then both of them started breathing heavily and Rebecca did a very girly gasp. And then as Alex was going close to her, Alex then felt something strange as his body was really getting cold and Alex started feeling his body begin to shut down very drastically "Alex are you alright. Baby talk to me!!! Alex!!!!, Alex!!!!" Rebecca said and then all of a sudden, Alex passed out in the water, and then Alex started drowning in the water and Rebecca dived under a water and then all of a sudden, her body started to shut down as well and then all of a sudden, the same people swam towards and it turned out unfortunately while Alex and Rebecca were under-water, the thugs were able to lightly stab them with a ruby jewel that had sleeping slime like liquid and it cause them to pass out or get killed in the process as well.

And then the thugs were able to grab Alex and Rebecca and they started taking them on a boat and the boat started taking them to Athens. And then later that day, Sadie and Spencer also noticed that both Alex and Rebecca were missing and right away they started looking for them all over the country. And then they even checked out of their hotel and started looking for them.

And then moments later, Alex and Rebecca slowly started to wake up and Alex noticed that both of them were inside of a freezing water and then Alex started hearing big time laughter and Alex knew right away if was Victoria Borodina and she was laughing like an evil witch "Good evening Mr. Aussmen" Victoria said "Borodina!!!!" Alex said in anger "when will you ever learn that I have people everywhere even in a country Greece. And also I know that I am getting closer to not only killing you but also steeling Sadie Holbrook's money and destroying the western world as well" Victoria said "Well kidnapping me and taking away my clothes is not going to change anything" Alex said "Oh yes you are correct little boy. Once I make a new European union, then it's off to Israel to try to do the same thing and blow up every country has any American influence and destroy them in everyway possible" Victoria said "And you see Alex, the communist will win the cold war and as for you, you will end up being a homeless person with no money what so ever" Victoria said "You know that's a complete fucking lie" Alex said with anger in his voice then Victoria then walked over to Alex touched his face and Alex could feel the cold and freezing glove that Borodina had and Alex started to shiver "Good-Bye Mr. Aussmen" Victoria said and then Victoria then left and her guards fallowed her and then Victoria went into an elevator and the elevator went up.

"Alex how in the world are we going to get out of here?" Rebecca asked and Rebecca was starting to get really scarred and then Alex then started freezing and thinking and then all of a sudden, Alex used all his strength and he was able break through some of the steel and then he climbed out of the water and he ran to the switch that was freezing the water and turned it off and then Rebecca climbed out "Oh Alex" Rebecca said and then all of a sudden, Alex noticed that this was not a normal building and it looked like the same building he saw when he was younger and it looked like the same medical building and then all of a sudden Alex herd Victoria's voice again "Good luck trying to escape Alex. I set the timer to 60 minutes and it's same obstacle course building that you had to go to when you were little. Only this time, you are timed very badly. Not enough time to escape" Victoria said and then Victoria did a very evil witch laugh and then all of a sudden, Rebecca and Alex started running and they then ran to a door and Alex open the door and he saw a lot of climbing elements and Alex and Rebecca started climbing really hard and they had to jump over different things and a lot of dangerous weapons were being thrown at them like crazy and they then ran more and more and then they found another door and as they were running there was trap doors that would appear and Alex would grab on the metal bars that were above his head and Alex would hold on for dear life and then as they got to the next part, it was even more dangerous and it was a path that also had traps but under them was a huge swimming full of great white sharks and Alex and Rebecca kept on going but then Rebecca felt the force of one of the flying objects hitting her and Alex grabbed on to her hand really tightly and Rebecca started crying and Alex was able to pull her in and Alex then hugged Rebecca really tightly in his arms and Alex felt Rebecca's naked body pressing towards him and Alex and Rebecca were able to get out of the building and they saw the ocean and they jumped off the building and building exploded into flames and they jumped into the water and Alex sadly got knocked out and Alex then began to sink really badly and more bad guys showed up and grabbed Rebecca and started taking her away and they were able to kidnap her.

And then 3 hours later, Alex was in the hospital in Athens and one of the doctors that was able to speak English recognized Alex from his face and was able to contact

Sadie and Spencer right away and they raced to the hospital and saw Alex "Alex are you alright?" Sadie asked and then Alex started moaning and then he saw Sadie's face and her blonde hair and her beautiful and gorgeous and stunning blue eyes "Where am I?" Alex asked "Your in Athens, one of the doctors called us and told Spencer and I that you were here" Sadie said "And Rebecca?" Alex asked "she sadly got kidnapped Alex" Spencer said, "Fuck!!!!" Alex said and then Alex started breathing very heavily "It's okay we are going to get her back man" Spencer said "It's okay, I may know where she is" Alex said "and I think you guys may need to go back to states right away" Alex said and then right away as Alex said that, more thugs came and a lot of chaos happened and all of a sudden, Borodina's thugs were able to break into the hospital and poison Sadie and Spencer really badly and were able to knock them out and kidnap them and also take them away, Alex then right away got out of the hospital bed and he was able to steel some normal doctor clothes and he started chasing the thugs and they had guns in their hands and they started shooting at Alex.

Alex then felt a grenade come towards him and a huge explosion happened and Alex saw Borodina's helicopter up in the air and Alex knew he must go to Ukraine and must defeat Victoria Borodina once and for all.

Chapter 4 Never Try to Kill a Ukraine Woman

As the explosions happened, Alex then started running and he found a car and he started heading towards the main airport in Greece. And even though Alex had no ID with him, he was able to memorize his ID and passport number with flying colors and also know his bank number as well. Alex then got through the customs really well. But then another strange thing happened where Alex fell through a trap door inside of the airport and Alex fell on a sofa under the airport in a strange and secret room and it Salem "I think I can help you defeat Borodina Alex. And your going to need my help getting into Ukraine" Salem said "Thank you. I really appreciate it a lot" Alex said "No problem Alex" Salem said and then all of a sudden, Salem was able to hand Alex one of his clothes and he was wearing normal 1980's clothes again and a door started to open a fighter airplane with blue and green and yellow was on the airplane and Alex climbed into the plane "There is a couple of things of thing you have to do before going to Borodina's castle in Ukraine. I will guide you through everything" Salem said "Sounds great thanks" Alex said and then as Alex climbed into the plane he then felt the power of the airplane "Alright Alex, now what you have to do is that Borodina is going steel a lot of money from all the countries that on the United States side and she will steel it using a satiate and you have to fire at all of them" Salem said "oh okay" Alex said

And then all of a sudden, Alex took off from Greece and Alex started flying all over the world and started heading east and Alex started seeing a lot of Borodina's satellites that had Ukraine colors on them and as Alex was getting closer, there all of a sudden was a lot of communist fighter planes that were firing and chasing Alex. And then Alex started firing a lot of missiles and gun bullets as well. And then would do a huge roll over on the plane and then Alex was able to fire at the communist airplanes and then all of a sudden a lot of Sandinista communist fighter planes also started showing up and firing at Alex and Alex then was able to fire around 99 missiles at the Sandinista airplanes and 900 fighter planes were firing at Alex non stop. Alex then kept on going and he fired more missiles and he was able to blow up satellites that were created by Victoria Borodina and destroy around 30 of them around different parts of the world. And then Alex kept on flying in the fighter plane and more Sandinista and communist jets kept on firing at him. And then kept firing a lot of missiles and rockets at the airplanes and then all of a sudden, Alex flew over the country of Ukraine and all of a sudden in the dark clouds and over the thunder and lighting, Alex saw Borodina's Ukraine castle that gray and black and had some communist colors and also some colors of the Ukraine flag all over it. "Alright Salem, I'm going in and I'm going to blow up the communist castle" Alex said "Alright be-careful Alex. And very soon I'm going to call the United States army and air-force to help you and we are going to take Borodina down buddy" Salem said "sounds great" Alex said

And then all of a sudden was able to find a landing spot in Ukraine and he saw more thunder and lighting all over the castle and Alex right away started running as fast as he could. And as Alex was going towards the castle himself he then ran into a couple of Ukraine guardsmen guarding Borodina's castle and the pointed their guns at Alex "Vin vy tut ne nalezhyte!!!!!!! Zupynyty!!!!!" and then all of a sudden with a lot of rage built up, Alex then pulled out a kitchen knife from his pocket and stabbed the guardsmen in the neck and blood started coming out and then more guardsmen showed up "Vbyvaty amerykans'kykh!!!!" and then Alex took out a handgun and he was able to shoot 50 bullets at different times and shot the guardsmen in the heads and then Alex was able to get into the castle and he blew up one of the main door and sneaked in. And then all of a sudden, Alex saw Borodina in a very queen like outfit with one side of her queen with the Sandinista colors and then the other side was communist USSR colors as well "Very soon. Once I still all of Ms. Holbrock's money I will be the new queen of the world and I will blow up every leader's home and kill of them, and I will create the Borodina Empire and nobody will be able to stop me. Not even the stupid Americans" Borodina said in a very evil feminine voice and then all of a sudden as she kept on walking she saw a Queen Crown with blue, red, black colors with diamonds and rubies and gold jewelry on it. And Borodina grabbed the crown and put it on her head and in her room she also had computers that showed much money that she had. But worst of all in the room, Sadly Rebecca and Sadie were in huge containers of water and both of the girls were butt naked and Borodina had a remote in her hand that controlled the tempter and then also different advanced wires that were going to suck up a lot of information they had from the brain. "Oh Sadie, I knew this day would come where my own people would get revenge on your people for becoming good friends with all of the royal family and taking everything from the Ukraine and if you can't tell I also despised your mother and father as well in the shadows" Borodina said in a very evil witch like voice and then Borodina walked over to Rebecca and Rebecca sadly had very sad puppy dog like eyes and she banged on the tank a couple of times "I have seen this type of look before. And this is what little boy Alex looked like before I told him the truth about me back in 1976. And now only with you I will kill you and steel your money and I will use your DNA to make me young again and make myself beautiful again....MUAHAHAHAHAHAHAHAHAHAHAHAHAHAHAHAHAHAHAHAHAHAHAHAHAHAHA" Borodina laughed and then all of a sudden Alex had a very angry look on his face and then he broke through the doors and he pointed his gun at Borodina "It's all over Borodina. Your under arrest!!!!!!" Alex said "Ahhhhhh Mr. Aussmen!!!! I am very glad you are here. It's pitty that I didn't kidnap you once again and put in the water with Ms. Olga and Ms. Holbrook as well. And then as for Spencer, he is also here as well" Borodina said all of a sudden Borodina pressed a button on her remote and all of a sudden Spencer was then tied up in ropes and he was about to be lowered to grinder and Spencer was scarred out of his mind and screaming "With Spencer I'm going to drop him into a grinder where not only will his balls and penis get destroyed but his whole body will get destroyed as well little boy" Borodina said "And then you won't be able to save either of them because I will be the queen of the world and start a new dynasty and a new empire and destroy the west once and for all" Borodina said and then all of a sudden Borodina grabbed a giant queen staff "And this time unlike the past, he will not inter-fear with my plans this time Mr. Aussmen!!!!!" Borodina said "and also you will now for once pay the price of being a hero of the west Mr. Aussmen!!!!!!...."Borodina said in a very witch like voice and then all of a sudden Borodina grabbed her staff and pointed the staff and killed one of her own guardsmen and then Borodina smiled like the evil queen from snow white and hey ugly yellow teeth were showing and she yelled "GOOD BYE MR. AUSSMEN!!!!!!!!.....AND IT'S TIME THAT YOU DIE AND GO TO HELL!!!!!!" Borodina yelled and then all of a sudden Borodina then started firing a lot of missiles and exploding liquid and causing explosions all over her castle and then Alex got forced against the wall and then more of Borodina's decorations started falling on Alex and Alex felt the pain very badly. And then Borodina started screaming in angry and she started screaming and yelling more and more like a witch and throwing more staff attacks at Alex and then Borodina hit Alex in the head and hit him in the stomach and stabbed Alex in the chest and Alex yelled in pain and blood started coming out and Alex got the knife out of his chest and then Alex kicked Borodina in the face and he grabbed a knight sword and Alex threw a lot of sword attacks and then Alex gave Borodina a cut on her arm and then Borodina then grabbed 30 grenades and threw 30 of them at Alex causing a lot of explosions and her castle started to catch on fire and Alex then got forced to the ground and Borodina yelled again and tried to stab Alex in the head with her queen staff and she kept on yelling and screaming very violently and then all of a sudden found a wine bottle and hit Borodina in the face and nose broke off of her face and blood started coming out and then Borodina grabbed Alex by the neck and started chocking him and stabbing in the neck with her dirty and her long witch like finger nails and then Alex was able to swing his body and all of a sudden was able to kick Borodina in the face and forced her to the ground and then all of a sudden Borodina got even more angry and grabbed her queen staff and then Alex was able to see a metal fireplace fork and Alex grabbed the item and then whacked Borodina with two hands and hitting her like a golf ball and then all of a sudden there was 99 United States Helicopters and army tanks and air force and military and then all of a sudden an army solider showed up and he spoke inside of a blow horn "THIS IS THE UNITED STATES ARMY AND THE AIR FORCE, WE KNOW THAT YOU ARE A COMMUNIST AND WORKING FOR THE RUSSIANS AND FOR THE SANDINSTAS IN NICARAGUA!!!!!! AND IF YOU DO NOT COME OUT, WE WILL FIRE AT YOUR CASTLE BLOW UP THE CASTLE AS WELL!!!!!!!!" the solider said

But it just didn't really mater as Borodina kept on attacking Alex with her staff and Alex just getting more and more hurt during the fight as well. And then Alex had around 6 different cuts around his body and then Borodina did more attacks at Alex and then all of a sudden Alex was able to dodge one of her attacks and then grabbed the staff and kicked Borodina in the face and then Alex grabbed another wine bottle whacked Borodina in the face and then Alex punched Borodina in the face with no remorse and then Borodina tried to stab Alex with a sword and then Alex kicked Borodina in the face and knocked her to the ground "WHY YOU LITTLE FOOL!!!!!" Borodina said in anger and then all of a sudden Alex saw a bucket of chemicals and then Alex poured the pocket of chemicals and all of a sudden all of Borodina's long hair started coming off of her and her skin started getting older and older and Borodina started screaming and then Borodina grabbed her queen crown tried to stab Alex with her crown and her queen staff and then all of a sudden Alex grunted his teeth and anger tackled Borodina to the ground and Alex with all his might and his strength started chocking her and Borodina started screaming pain and then Alex then grabbed the knight sword and then stabbed her in the forehead and then more of her skin and her blood started dying as then all of a sudden Borodina's body and her head started turning into a skull and into a skeleton's body and Victoria Borodina was dead.

And then all of a sudden Alex started running to the tank and he was able to disable everything on the keyboards and then water was dumped on the ground "Oh Alex" Rebecca said and then Alex also hugged Sadie as well "I'm glad you guys are alright" Alex said and then all of a sudden Alex then pressed another button and was able to save Spencer "thanks buddy, I really thought I was going to be dead meat" Spencer said "Your welcome Spencer" Alex said and then all three of them were able to find their clothes and all of a sudden they started running out Borodina's castle and there were a lot of explosions. And then all of a sudden as they got out of the castle, Alex then turned back and he saw Borodina's Ukraine castle on fire and started falling to the ground and then there was another explosion that happened as well.

And then all of a sudden, during that same night, Alex, Sadie, Rebecca, and Spencer were then taken to the United States embassy in Ukraine and Salem started handling everyone's paper work as well. "Alright guys, I was able to do your paper work and the good news is that you guys can go back to the states. And the army and everything else about Victoria Borodina will be investigated" Salem said "Thanks Salem" Alex said and then after that visit, they all then started heading to the airport and heading back to the United States and going through customs and immigration through New York City and through Newark, New Jersey and then as they were in the airport, Alex then was finally happy to have real American food and he got himself a Wendy's triple cheeseburger and a Dr. Pepper and some fries and then after he was done eating, he then used a napkin and whipped his face clean and then he went into the bathroom and used water to clean his face as well. And then after he was done doing that, he then went back to his seat and sat down "hopefully Borodina didn't do too much damage to you Sadie" Alex said "oh are you kidding Alex, my money is completely saved and in fact, I know have 99 trillion dollars in my bank account because of all the stocks my dad invested as well." Sadie with a huge smile on her face "So are you still going to keep doing this secret agent stuff Alex. Cause I think it maybe time for you to settle down, you just been on the run from life for a long time" Sadie said "I don't know" Alex said "come on Alex, you can start investing in stocks and making a lot of money, and you can live in a house like a normal person" Sadie said "I'm never going to be a normal person, my life is very fucked up and it will always be fucked up" Alex said "Plus I mean I can be around to help you Alex and be a good influence as well. I can imagine you have lacked that for a long time" Sadie said

And then later that day, Alex then headed back to Seattle, Washington and Sadie and Spencer headed back to Minnesota. And Alex was just tired and just really burned out from everything and all the missions he did and how he was almost 30 years old. And thought about what Sadie said to him and really he had nothing to loose, he just killed Borodina and with the cold war on the brink of being over, Alex then made the choice in his head that he will maybe not retire but just start settling down with someone.

As the plane landed in Seattle, Alex was able to grab a taxi back to his pen house apartment in Seattle, and when he got home, Alex then started looking his bank account and right away he went to stock market place in Seattle and they talked about which companies had a lot in shares and Alex started investing 9,000$ in buying shares around the millions and he started growing his money a lot more. And right away, Alex then started looking for some houses and he then was able to find a mansion in Kent, WA and around that point Alex had around 9,000,000 million dollars built up in stocks and he moved into his new mansion that had both a basketball court and also a tennis court and also a hot tub and a swimming pool that was both an indoor and outdoor pool. And then as he moved into his new house, he then quit working at Seattle Agencies and Alex professionally retired as a secret agent. And then Alex was able to give Jenny a phone call and Jenny was able to drive to Alex's new mansion in Kent and they both had a really wonderful time and even went skinny dipping in Alex's new pool and then watched movies wearing ropes and made out on Alex's couch "Oh I am really glad that you invited me to come Alex" Jenny said "Yeah me too. Anyway the reason I wanted to invite you to my house is because I really love you Jenny and I wanted to ask you...Will you marry me?" Alex asked and then Jenny just really smiled and she then said yes to Alex and then days later Alex and Jenny got married and their weeding was at Alex's new mansion in Kent, WA and a lot of people that Alex knew came to his weeding and their honey moon was in Brazil and then also Alex and Jenny both traveled the world and then they went to beaches and then to other parts of the world as well. And then during the trip they then were able to catch up with Sadie and Spencer in Italy and also travel with them as well to other places as well.

And then as Alex and Jenny's honeymoon was over, Alex then days later got a letter from Sadie saying that she moved back to Seattle and she lives in a new house that is very castle like. And then as they got the letter, Alex and Jenny then went to Sadie and Spencer's new castle like house in Kirkland and it was a very causal party with Alex drinking a beer and having steak and salad with ranch and mashed potatoes as well. And during the visit Alex took look around the house, Alex started having flash backs to Morella's house in Edmonds and that the house itself was very similar to Morella's house accept however it was more castle like then golden mansion, Alex also saw more English culture and paintings all over the house and Alex just sat down on a sofa and he saw a Dr. Pepper drink and he felt more relaxed then ever before in his life. And then all of a sudden, Jenny was able to find Alex and then Alex and Jenny started making out on the sofa and they started laughing and kissing each other on the lips "Oh Alex" Jenny said

www.ingramcontent.com/pod-product-compliance
Lightning Source LLC
Chambersburg PA
CBHW080749250626
47162CB00010B/3079